4

Harris, Elizabeth,
  1944-

The ant generator.

$22.95

DATE			

~~14 DAYS~~ - NOT RENEWABLE

BAKER & TAYLOR BOOKS

The Ant Generator

The John Simmons Short Fiction Award

The Ant Generator

ELIZABETH HARRIS

UNIVERSITY OF IOWA PRESS

IOWA CITY

University of Iowa Press, Iowa City 52242
Printed in the United States of America
First edition, 1991

In slightly different forms, "Hybrid Wolfdogs," "The World Record Holder," "The Grand Duke of Redonda," "The Catfish-Head Tree," and "Coming into Rio Harbor" first appeared in, respectively, the *Kansas Quarterly*, *Southwest Review*, *Antioch Review*, *Wind*, and *Shenandoah*, and "The World Record Holder" was reprinted in *New Stories from the South: The Year's Best, 1986*, ed. Shannon Ravenel (Chapel Hill, N.C.: Algonquin Books, 1986).

Printed on acid-free paper

The publication of this book is supported by a grant from the National Endowment for the Arts in Washington, D.C., a federal agency.

Library of Congress Cataloging-in-Publication Data
Harris, Elizabeth, 1944–
The ant generator/Elizabeth Harris.—1st ed.
p.   cm.
ISBN 0-87745-342-X (cloth)
I. Title.
PS3558.A64444A5   1991   91-17231
813'.54—dc20   CIP

With thanks to those who have helped me

Contents

The Ant Generator

The whole thing looked like a primitive drum—the head made out of leather or rubber tied down with several passes of small cord—and over the head, in all directions, swarmed ants. It was the ant generator. She was the inventor, and looking at it, she understood its worth. She had dreamed it in the last moment before waking and had brought it up with her out of her sleep.

She rolled over and embraced her husband Dan. Every morning when they first woke up, they hugged. He felt good to her in his cotton pajamas, and there was something reassuring about a man who slept in pajamas. She herself didn't wear anything to sleep in, though she thought she ought to.

She said, "I invented the ant generator."

While Dan was in the shower, she knelt naked by the bed on the new wall-to-wall carpet and prayed for the victims of hunger, sickness, injustice, and oppression. This gave her a feeling of doing something about those things. Afterwards she made the bed, tucking everything in neatly.

"It was to generate electrical power," she was saying. Husband and wife sat at the chrome and glass table. Dan had one long hand up to the wrist in the box of Bran Buds and was feeling around for the prize, which was supposed to be a toy gyroscope. Sylvia was slicing half a banana, pulling a tableknife towards her thumb in rapid strokes so that the slices of banana flipped over the knife into her bowl of cereal.

"There was some way, something in the drumhead, or underneath, that converted the scurrying of the ants into electrical power."

Dan pulled the plasticized paper package out of the cereal box and smiled. He looked like a kid, with his warm tan face, his round brush of black curls.

He poured milk from a half-gallon cardboard carton onto his bowl of cereal and banana and sat there with his spoon poised in his hand, considering. His cereal was getting soggy, but he liked it that way.

"Nope," he said seriously. "Can't be done." Dan was a computer programmer and got to be the hard science expert in the family, but unlike some of his science friends, he never condescended to Sylvia about such topics.

He ate some Bran Buds and banana, still thinking. Then he said, "Not unless there's some way to line the ants up. Organize their disorganized expenditure of energy along a single axis." He took another spoonful and added around it, "We don't know how to convert the random to the unidirectional."

Except in her dream, Sylvia had not thought of the ant generator as an actual invention: it was just an idea. She ate her cereal and banana.

"But if you could," Dan said, "if you could"—he looked at her with wide black eyes—"it would solve a lot of problems!"

After he finished his cereal, he opened the plasticized paper package and took out the small metal gyroscope. It was smaller than the picture on the box, but when he gave it a twist and let it go on the tabletop it stood upright, spinning, and moved in a straight line across the glass, spinning, spinning, until it reached the edge and dropped off.

Up to the end, the day went better than Sylvia expected. Lawrence, her boss at the small anthropological museum, did not come in, so she spent the day peacefully labeling axes and choppers and dart points and drills of the people called Archaic. How hard it was, she thought, to reconstruct much about them from such of their objects as we happened to find. It was like one of those connect-the-dots puzzles, except that, connected, the dots did not necessarily make a recognizable picture.

The museum was at the site of a famous dig, miles out of town. Sylvia left, as usual for Mondays, at four-thirty. From the black look of the cloud pile ahead, she would run through a rainstorm on the way. She had driven maybe a third of the distance back to town, the traffic still light at that hour so far out. Later she remembered that there were no other cars around her.

Suddenly, with a loud crack, the passenger window exploded into the right-hand side of the car. She remembered only a plowed field off in that direction, with trees and a house way on the other side. She saw nobody, no rock that might've been thrown, nothing from a slingshot. Maybe her own wheel, she thought—but afterwards Dan said it could not've popped a pebble up with enough force, not at that angle.

"Oh, baby!" he said, "Oh, baby!" They were standing inside the open door of the partly furnished apartment—she had told him about it all in a rush as she came in—and he had to hunch over to embrace her, he was so much taller than she was.

Down in the apartment house parking lot, he searched the seat and the floor of the car, pawing among the little rounded fragments, brushing them carelessly out of the black carpet, out onto the asphalt of the parking lot with his large hands. Here and there, a few substantial chunks, webbed finely with cracks, were still held together by the sticky laminate. He slipped his hands down behind the seat, underneath it, in the front and in the back, felt and brushed, neverminding that he pricked himself on a sharp point here and there. He pulled the black rubber mat off the floor in front and shook it. But there was nothing except pieces of glass and some dirt, an empty matchbook, a few dry leaves.

"Something that hit and bounced off," he said grimly. "A pellet gun. A BB wouldn't do it, from that distance." It was the only explanation he could figure.

"Kids," he said, "picking a car going past."

"And it was mine," she marveled.

He said she was lucky—they were lucky—it hadn't been a .22, which would've gone on through and hit her: she could've cracked up the car and been killed. He might never have even known what had happened.

"Oh, baby," he said, and enfolded her again there in the parking lot by the open door of the car. They stood surrounded by the little fragments of glittering glass.

But what she could not stop thinking about was how one moment the passenger window had been a complete, rolled-up sheet that would keep out wind and rain, whereas the next moment the front half of it had been blown away into strangely shaped fragments and the back half shattered into a useless web of cells, already sagging inward, beginning to fold down in big pieces. She could not comprehend it in some way: how it was possible or what it meant. She had not been able to when it had happened, though all the same, she had driven straight on.

Patsy Soames's Ghost Story about Farley

You read in the paper where forty percent of Americans believe they've had contact with the dead, and you've got to be ready for anything. In my own opinion, though, it didn't really happen, not real-as-rocks. I'm not saying Patsy Soames made it up. I doubt she could've, and why would she? A little notoriety, chills and thrills? Hey, this is Patsy Soames, long-haul party girl, who's been having hers for twenty years and, in case that wears thin, has a nice law career—sleepy practice—and a decent second marriage to a man from our same crowd. So it didn't happen, this what-you-may-call-it of Farley, but she honestly thinks it did: that makes it a mental rather than a physical event.

Hallucination would at least seem to be a possibility. If you took a poll on the person among us most likely to pass out at a party, Patsy Soames would get her votes, for all the times those of us who can remember anything can remember her, face-down on a table at some club at 2 A.M., long freckled arms sprawled out in front of her; or Patsy Soames falling off the couch sideways at dawn in somebody's house out at the lake. But as a matter of fact, Patsy's nowhere near the hallucinating stage (we have friends who are, so we know what it looks like) and claims she was not drunk at the time.

I plump for another kind of mental phenomenon. Say a sort of waking dream, such as any of us might have when, in a low moment, the half thought rises up before you as a visible certainty. You know how it is when a person dies, especially under iffy circumstances: you wonder, was there something I did or didn't do? And then it might come to you so clearly you could see it. Not that I think Patsy Soames had anything particular to regret about Farley. She was no different to him than a lot of people, members of our moving, whiling party. Any of us could've seen him after he was dead (seen and forgotten, I'd say): Patsy's just blunt enough to remember.

But how this apparition came to her is not something Patsy

Soames troubles herself about. "I don't know," she says and passes a square hand over her eyes. "I really don't."

There she sits, feet up on a chair, some white-liquor drink in front of her. Quiet in here, the right side of midafternoon but not yet time for the after-work crowd. We often seem to be waiting for something.

"You haven't heard my ghost story?" she says. She laughs her melancholy horsy laugh.

And if you show interest in this sort of thing—not everybody does—she will tell you how she saw Farley after he was dead. It's something to talk about, even if there are people in our crowd who don't want to hear it anymore.

The bartender is cutting limes behind the bar; you can smell it. We're comfortable over here at the big round table in the corner.

Patsy Soames settles herself, leans a long freckled forearm on the table, and adopts an expression of explanation. "First," she says, "you have to understand how I met Farley." I think of Farley: our buddy, our pal, our ambiguous friend, who is dead.

"I first got to know Farley over a foot massage," she says, "in the Come-on-Downtown Lounge?" Like a lot of Texas women, Patsy Soames will sound a statement like a question. She flips her head to flip her hair out of her face, the short black Dutch-boy bob that takes all kinds of disarray and falls back into place the same. She is not a pretty woman, but she looks like somebody.

"This was a bar my then-husband then partly owned, which later was torn down to make room for one of those high-rise office buildings. And actually," she admits, "it wasn't much of a place. Small, narrow, dark, straight back from the street door, and papered in that godawful red velvet flocked wallpaper? But it had a clientele: they booked in music acts at night." She takes a sip of her drink and sets the glass back down carefully in the same wet ring on the napkin.

"Well, this particular night," says Patsy Soames, "the place was packed, and I was sitting up by the street door with my shoes off and my feet up on one of the only empty chairs in the joint, knowing I'd have to give it up to the first person that looked at it, when in comes fat Farley in a white shirt and tie. God knows why—I think this was after he quit his job.

"I knew him around town. We all did, but I don't think I'd ever had a conversation with him.

"He said something like, 'May I have that chair?' And I suppose he made even that sound pompous, because that was the way Farley was when he didn't know you well.

"I said he could—wobbly old bentwood chair—and moved one foot at a time. 'But I want you to know it's a sacrifice,' I said, 'cause I just spent the whole day on my feet running around the courthouse.'

"'Well, leave 'em up there,' Farley said. 'Put 'em on my lap and I'll give you a foot massage.' And I did and he did, and it was a good un, on the high cushion of his thighs. Afterwards I felt like I had new feet."

Patsy Soames raises her glass for a moment, to new feet, perhaps, or the memory of Farley as masseur; then she takes a drink. There's a window in this corner, but blinded. If you get stuck at the wrong angle, the brightness of the hot harsh street outside slices in on you from around the window frame. In here, we are dim and cool at least.

"It was the beginning of my friendship with Farley," Patsy Soames says.

There is a medium-long pause. She says, "I suppose you have to know a bit about Farley." There is a longer pause, in which I am thinking the essential thing she does not want to say about our dead friend Farley. And I recall, for instance, how he liked to say he had been in the CIA or something in Vietnam—"Intelligence," he said, and looked important and looked away—but we never knew whether to believe him.

Patsy Soames shakes her head and smiles a little, having recalled a nice way not to say that Farley was a notorious liar.

"He held himself like Alfred Hitchcock in the old TV titles," she says, "and was known to say anything for effect.

"Like," she goes on, "I remember this. 'You *know*,' Farley said one time, in the way that meant he did and you didn't, 'the real reason the Japanese bombed Pearl Harbor. It was because Roosevelt used the wrong Japanese verb to the Japanese ambassador.'

"And Farley told this story about how of course Roosevelt hadn't known any Japanese, but he had memorized this one phrase, which unfortunately had contained the wrong verb form, which had made the phrase into a terrible insult."

It was the kind of story Farley liked to tell, in which someone else, with grave consequences, had not known something that Farley himself knew.

Patsy Soames laughs a little again, in a sad way, and her heavy hair falls over one eye; she tosses her head to fling it back. "I suppose Farley did know some Japanese. I think he had a degree in Asian Studies, something like that. Maybe he had an M.B.A., too. But what he said, it was all bullshit. He just made it up, and everybody knew it.

"So somebody who was a World War II buff would catch him out, if they bothered. And Farley would do a little sidestep and make up some more. Like, he would say how this information had indeed been concealed from the public and even from the community of scholars, but had long been the property of the intelligence community."

Patsy Soames drains her drink, waves to the bartender for another one. "He was fun though," she says. "He always had something to say, even if it was all bullshit. Better bullshit than something serious, for chrissake."

We all feel that way. Remember Conduct, on your report card? Our friends all cheerfully flunk "Uses time wisely."

"And Farley was generous," Patsy Soames adds. "When we first knew him he was working for the Pharmacy Control Board or some such bureaucracy, and he used to show up in the bars after work wearing a three-piece suit with his pockets full of pills, which he passed out by handfuls to anybody who wanted them."

The bartender, a man with very round, light eyes, brings Patsy's drink. "Thanks, Marvin," Patsy says—no need to tell him to put it on her tab.

She drinks, considering how to proceed, for as many times as she has told this story, she tells it a little different every time. She puts the glass down exactly in the damp ring on the new napkin, leans her freckled arm against the edge of the table.

"Farley," she pronounces carefully, "became a sort of institution." She has skipped over the time at first when people did not trust him, when they thought he might just be setting you up with the pills to get you busted if you stood out next to the dumpster passing a joint around or went off to the restroom to chop coke on the back of the toilet.

"I suppose it was because after he quit his job, he was always around." Farley had quit his job and left his wife all on the same day and never went back to the big mortgaged house in the hills except to pick up some clothes.

"He lived in his car for a while, a little white wire-wheeled Triumph that he later sold. After that he usually had a place to stay, but he never seemed to spend much time there. He was always in public. You would see him coming out of the library with a stack of spy novels or sitting in an outdoor cafe reading.

"Or he would be in the bars." Patsy intones in a dreary sing-song, "Sundays, Thanksgivings, Christmases. New Year's Day. If there wasn't a party or a barbecue everybody was invited to. Fourth of July, Memorial Day, Labor Day. All the days you're supposed to spend with your family if you have one but might not want to even if you do?" Here I suppose she alludes to her own first marriage, which was falling apart around that time.

"So you could always find him," she says, "if you couldn't find anybody else."

It was true: we let him entertain us until it became his function to. And yet, I think that was more Farley's fault than ours. Plenty of strangers have showed up at our ongoing party— a certain unease elsewhere, the only admission—and now sit here as friends. But Farley seemed to think he had to tap-dance to get in, and so he did.

As to why he left his job and his wife and the big mortgaged house in the hills to come dancing after us, the only explanation he ever offered was that it had all been "too much." And he said this casually, with a delicate wave of his fat hand, as if we who were dedicated to taking everything lightly, lightly, must surely understand.

"He was popular in a way," Patsy Soames reflects, "even with people who didn't actually like him." Then she adds quickly, "Though I liked him. We were good buddies," and, finger along her naked lip, trails off into memory.

She does not say how good buddies. The truth is that at some point she and Farley became lovers, of a sort. It was not, as the phrase ran, serious. For, surprisingly, Farley—bald, big-bellied, pompous Farley—was lovers more or less simultaneously with a number of women in our crowd, as they all knew. It came out in jokes, the casual remark, little glances and grins. Unattached or otherwise attached women, good-looking or ordinary-looking women, younger women, older women. It amazed the men in our crowd who knew, but among the women Farley had the reputation of a terrific lover. Maybe it was the massage. Also, in spite of all the other lies he told, apparently he was honest about whatever he offered. He didn't fall in love or expect women to. He didn't expect them to pay for things. And he did not leave one for another but moved among them as among friends. In my own observation, he was more comfortable with women than with men and cultivated them with more dignity.

"Of course," Patsy Soames sighs and plunges in on another side of Farley's popularity, "there was his coke dealing. But," she says earnestly, "we liked him, those of us who did like him, before he dealt coke." She takes another swig of her drink.

"And it wasn't as if he set out to deal," which was true. Farley, after he left his job, had set out to do nothing but what came to him minute by minute, up on the surface of his days. "It was just," Patsy Soames says, lifting her thick fingers off the table in the slightest gesture, "by going from one thing to another that he ended up walking around with a sandwich baggie full of white powder in his jacket pocket."

The bartender turns on the ceiling fans, and though we are already air-conditioned, a little breeze is nice. We turn our faces to the ceiling for a moment.

Then Patsy sighs again and goes on. "I was seeing a good deal of him there at the end. My first husband and I had broken up, and I'd knock off work early, the winter afternoons coming down, and go in for a drink to a big bar and restaurant some friends of ours owned, who had given Farley a job managing it when he got to needing one badly. So he would always be there, and later we might eat together, if neither of us had anything else to do."

While Patsy speaks, I see Farley the way he was that last winter, sitting at the end of the bar in the still nearly empty afternoons, wearing maybe an old crewneck and a pair of corduroy pants. In between whatever else he had to do, he would be reading the paper and sipping on a Dos Equis. That was his drink. He was a light drinker—I never saw him drunk.

"'Hi, there,' he would say, like he said to everybody. And I'd sit down and order a drink. And he'd ask me how my day had been, and I'd say something, and he'd say things that showed he was listening.

"Like, I remember this. 'Ouch,' he'd say, if you told him something unpleasant that happened to you. 'That must've hurt.' And, I don't mean he wasn't sympathetic, but it was like a course he had taken one time, Active Listening? In which you learned the right rigmarole to say to keep people talking? Because he could only care pro forma, if you know what I mean. He might even be sneaking a look at the paper at the same time.

"But"—she leans over and her black hair flops in her face—"that was the point. I might be too. Because"—she speaks from behind the soft wall of her hair—"you know, about ninety-five percent of the time that's all you can take from people?" She leans back, tosses her head to toss her hair back, and it's true. We pass the time huddled around tables together, the same people, day after year, but that doesn't mean we can take each other at any great intensity.

Patsy Soames swallows the rest of her drink all at once and orders another one. "Or," she goes on in a more normal way, "we'd talk some nonsense, like Farley did.

"And I remember," she says, "one afternoon in that last winter of his life, I was sitting on a barstool leaning on that padded thing they put up on the edge of the bar to keep us drunks from pulling our drinks off, and Farley and I got to talking—I don't know how it came up—about ambition in life and whether you had one. Maybe it was something in the horrorscopes."

The round-eyed bartender, making Patsy's drink, looks as if he might be listening, but this is just the way Marvin looks.

"And Farley said, in his well-it's-all-bullshit-anyway manner, 'What's your ambition in life?' For something to talk about, you know, like he did.

"Understand, I'm sitting there with a drink in front of me, but somehow it came to me to say, 'I think I'd like to meet a man who didn't drink.'" She whinnies. And maybe that remark at the time was an allusion to her then-becoming-ex-husband, not that her present husband is much different in that respect.

Marvin, still wearing his expression of perpetual interest, brings the drink; the prevailing opinion is that Marvin is interested in very little.

"Well," Patsy says, "after Farley and I finished our laugh, I said, 'How about you?' I mean, did he have an ambition, you know.

"And Farley, in that same well-let's-talk-this-shit-anyway man-

ner, said oh, he'd like to make a something-figure coke deal.
Surprised me, but I guess I figured he was about as serious as
I was. I knew he was dealing. All our friends knew—they were
who he was dealing to. But it was just another buzz. Nobody
got into real trouble with it. And Farley did just *say* things.
Later, you realize."

She shakes her head, remembering, and takes a big drink of
her drink. This time, too, she puts it down as carefully as she
did before, in the damp ring that's already on the little napkin.
It takes a lot to get Patsy Soames drunk.

"After Farley ran away, and even after he was dead," she says,
"for months afterwards, the owners would find those little zip-
per bank bags with one or another day's receipts that Farley
should've taken to the bank stuffed here and there in cabinets
and drawers in the office. They thought he must've been too
out of it to know what he was doing by then. But what I
thought, when I heard that, was, he was stashing money for the
something-figure coke deal."

Patsy leaves it at that, without going into how Farley could've
stolen from his friends, who had given him a job when he
needed it. My own opinion is that nobody was as much Farley's
friend as they might've believed, though I take this for Farley's
misfortune more than anybody else's. Also, of course, Farley
would've thought he could get away with it, that they would
never find him out, or he could tidy things up somehow, if
they did.

"Then one day," Patsy Soames says and passes a hand over
her eyes, "Farley walked into the little windowless office in the
back and saw the partners sitting over the books."

There is a long pause, in which we all contemplate retribu-
tion dangling over Farley, though it came down years ago.

"He ran away," she says, staring off over your shoulder as if
she expects to see him there. "Later we found out he went to
Oklahoma City. I think he had a woman friend there, but if he
had, either he never found her or she couldn't help him."

There is another pause. Patsy would skip this part if she

could, but you can't have a ghost until you've got a dead person. "Well," she says finally, "you can guess how it was for him. Out of money, out of coke, out of friends, in a room at the Holiday Inn in Oklahoma City. Come crashing down off it all."

She drinks from her drink, says, "He never expected to make old bones."

She pauses again, goes on. "They said he took a bath first, as if he was planning to do it in the tub, but then he didn't. Maybe he had a thought about them finding him there, naked in gore and shit. He was a clean man. Or maybe he meant to spare the maid. It would've been like him.

"So he got out, they said, and shaved and put on a three-piece suit before he slit his wrists lengthwise, the way they do when they mean it."

And listening to this, I can't keep from seeing Farley's turned-back white shirt cuffs, with his blood on them, also blood making a track on the white tile of the bathroom floor, disappearing into the dark carpet of the room, because all of those rooms have dark carpets, to hide the things people do there.

"Afterwards," Patsy Soames says bleakly, "they said he might've been euphoric. He rang the desk to say he was coming down, then walked out the door of the room carrying an attaché case and collapsed and died. That's what we heard anyway."

The street door blasts open and a couple of people come in. Patsy Soames squints at the light and shudders and looks away.

She says, "He never left a note or anything. They traced him here from his address book. In the end they shipped him back to wherever he was from, to be cremated."

Dallas, I heard. One of those glazed treeless suburbs that people fight to get into, and out of.

You stir in your chair. You are ready for Farley's ghost. Patsy Soames drinks from her drink, shrugs a shoulder. "We waked him in the bar," she says. "I went. Everybody went. Then we just sat around and looked at each other. I don't know." She passes a hand over her eyes. "It was too much."

I'll say. Nobody wanted to talk about it, of course, and it was hard to talk about anything else. Everybody was pissed off at him for stealing from his friends, for inviting death in among us—inviting it!—and for putting himself where they couldn't feel right about being pissed off at him. And that Farley, of all people, had done this. We sat in the bar and waked him, but we might as well've been on the street.

"I didn't stay," Patsy Soames says. "I couldn't stand it. I had a couple of drinks and left. But that might've been where I picked him up, if that's the way it happened." She gets this faraway look on her face: destination, spook city.

"I felt kind of bad about leaving so soon, but you know, I just wanted to get the whole thing over with. I think that was why I started talking to him in the car. Not," she glances over at you, "that I believe in any of that stuff. Even now.

"I said to him, 'Farley, I'm sorry you're dead. I'm gonna miss you.' There I was in my ten-year-old Honda with the oxidized finish, cruising down Pecan Street at the speed that lets you make all the lights. And maybe it was about then I began to feel like he heard me, but I didn't take it seriously. I went on, though. I said, 'I'm sorry I couldn't stick your wake any longer, and I wish you hadn't killed yourself at all. But if that's what you wanted to do with your life, it's all right with me.' And saying it seemed to make it true, though I hadn't thought about it before.

"I went on over to Rona Selden's? She was just getting divorced at the time, too. I think we were going out to eat or something." Patsy Soames takes a drink of her drink and puts it down, still carefully in the wet ring on the napkin.

"So I go in at Rona's, which is, you know, the kind of furnished one-room apartment you get if you can't afford much rent and don't want to take a lease? With the avocado shag carpet? And the doors that open out onto the courtyard, with the empty swimming pool full of leaves. Rona's all right"—Patsy looks at me, because Rona is also one of us—"and Rona'll swear to everything I say insofar as she saw it."

The street door opens again, and three people come in wearing work clothes. In the bars where we go, they don't put clocks, but it must be almost five o'clock.

"Well," Patsy says, "we're sitting there watching the news on television with the sound turned off—believe me, it's the only way—and I have my feet up on this dicky little coffee table they have there.

"And in comes Farley! Through the door, which is shut! Just fades in and comes across the room, not what you'd call continuously—in flashes. I got a flash of him coming through and another halfway across the room. And he was wearing the three-piece suit, gray pinstripe, with a white shirt and tie. No wounds or blood on him. He looked—I don't know how to describe it—eager, flirting his fat body, if you can call it a body. He flickers over to me, sits down on the coffee table, and bends over to take his shoes and socks off. Heavy black wing tips. Long black socks. And I know what he wants before he puts his bare ghost-feet in my lap: he wants me to give him a foot massage! Why me? Maybe because of what I said to him in the car about letting him go: maybe he thought if I'd give him that I'd give him this, too.

"And at the time, I thought, why not? I mean, I'd've given Farley a foot massage alive, so I put my hands where I saw his pale bare feet and tried. But you know, there was nothing there. For the casual kindness of skin, nothing at all."

Patsy Soames takes a drink from her drink, shrugs. "Well," she says, "all this time Rona Selden is sitting there off to the side in her La-Z-Boy recliner, and she doesn't see Farley, but she sees me looking at something, then moving my hands around, and she says, 'What are you doing?'

"That broke it. Farley gets up, picks up his shoes and socks, gives me a sort of reproachful look, like I wouldn't do the one little thing he asked, and flashes back across the room the same way he came. The last I see of him is his fat butt flashing through the closed door."

We are all still there with Farley, flashing in timeless light where, no matter the gestures of other people, whatever we want isn't quite available, either. The street door opens; more people come in. Traffic stinks and rumbles outside.

Hybrid Wolfdogs

Trumbo would not have gotten the wolfdogs to begin with if things had been going well for him in Texas. He had arrived from California on the real estate boom, had driven the taxicab-yellow El Camino across the desert from L.A. in a sort of—it turned out premature—ecstasy of achievement, as if he abolished the monotone distances with it. Then the boom went bust, and though he was still hanging on, he did not know for how long. He had a feeling, probably slop-over of paranoia, he told himself, that people he met did not like him. He was camping out between coming and maybe going in the model condo of a half-empty development he was partners in. And though he was no kid and no stranger to the ups and downs of business, it was an uncomfortable, nowhere, uncertain time for him, with not much to do.

To relax, he told himself, because he does not enjoy television, he drove. Folded his long body into the truck and just went—to San Antonio or Waco, or some name or no-name place he could turn around and head back from. Up on the interstate flying in a clear golden P.M., or down on the blacktop at night in a little rain, where he could watch for empty stretches and do stunts, hurtling around in bootlegger turns and four-wheel drifts, he seemed to leave his anxieties strung out along the road. Superstitious, he came back by a different route.

And it was on the way back from one of these getaways, barreling down a darkening alleyway of pines, that he saw the hand-lettered sign propped up between two rocks at the side of the road. It said HI-BRID (1/2) WOLF DOGS. Wolfdogs, he thought. He pulled off braking, sliding a curve in the gravel like an illegible signature, bumping up onto the weed-spiked concrete apron of a long burnt-out gas station. He unwound himself from inside the truck and got out, a tall, long-legged, gray-haired man in jeans and a cowboy shirt with pearl snaps. Then he reached back into the truck for his straw cowboy hat and put it on. In Texas he had started wearing cowboy clothes

2 5

and telling people he was from Oklahoma, a fact which had been true forty years before. His new cowboy boots echoed on the concrete. He walked loosely, the way he walked when he might buy something, but there was nobody around to see him. The blackened walls of the station had been streaked by seasons of rains; the windows were three-quarters boarded up with warped old sheets of plywood. He looked in over the top of one, and there they were, two of them, penned up and trotting nervously around and around inside the roofless shell.

The sight of them discouraged him at first. They were only half-grown, he figured; they were skinny and long-legged, with big feet and rough mixed-color coats. Still, he thought, wolfdogs, and how they would be better-looking older. He believed they would grow up like supercharged dogs. He walked on around the station, where he could see signs of a house through the trees, then went back to the truck and honked until a barrel-shaped shirtless man in overalls came around the station. He had kernels of corn stuck in an untrimmed brown beard, and he claimed to be selling the wolfdogs for his brother-in-law. A likely strategy, Trumbo thought. But after some discussion, he bought the dogs cheap enough.

Only after he had them tied down and shivering in the back of the truck did his doubts return and magnify. Those wolfdogs were unpromising-looking creatures, and he wondered if he had sold them to himself, as he is liable to do with things. He did not really know anything about dogs, having spent most of his adult life doing things with machinery and real property. He would have to find a place to board them, spend more money—he could not keep them but a night or two in the little patio of the model condo.

Afterwhile, though, his fit of buyer's remorse spent itself, and he thought how, for all of that, he had bought them, and how fine they would be, trained up right. He did have a place in mind where he might get a deal on keeping them, and he *could* afford a hobby. It would be cheaper than all that gaso-

line. Indeed, an inexpensive hobby was exactly what a man in
his position needed. Too, he told himself, a man from Oklahoma even ought to raise dogs, though he did not actually
recall that they had had dogs when he lived in Oklahoma. The
only thing he remembered at all about animals from those
days was from the blacksmith shop where the uncle who had
raised him had shod mules and plowhorses, and they could
give you a good swift kick if you weren't watching, but this did
not seem to apply to dogs.

And in fact, he succeeded in boarding them at the place he
had remembered, not a regular kennel, just a little property
he had seen where the man had a pen that might hold them.
Tucked down in a little valley, looking up at a new subdivision
all around, the place looked, Trumbo thought, like all the
places of those people look. Derelict cars outside, wheelless
and unhooded, pieces of scrap iron, an ancient iron harrow
like a huge rusty insect. Alongside, under a spreading live oak,
ran the pen, built partly out of an old billboard. It had once
held goats.

Then Trumbo gave up driving and spent his afternoons and
evenings down in the little valley with the dogs, where the
light seemed to get soaked up a good half hour before it
evaporated off the hills. There he jerked the dogs around on
long ropes, as he had found out you were supposed to do.
Evening after summer evening, he tied them to the ropes, let
them wander away from him in the long pen, then whistled
and reeled them in, whistled and reeled them in. Sometimes
as he did this he thought about the value of perseverance, how
you could do a lot of things if you stuck to them long enough,
and about his whole long life of hard work and self-denial.
This line of thought might lead him to remember his aunt who
had raised him in Oklahoma, a tall rawboned woman in a
homemade housedress, saying, "Donnie can do anything."
That was him.

Right down on it, he would think about the apartment building that he still owned in Santa Monica, and he would feel reassured that things would work out for him in Texas if he just kept making the right motions.

Back behind, in front of an old yellow housetrailer with one end swallowed up by an unpainted shack, an old man sat by the door, watching doubtfully. Should've sold that land a year ago, Grandpaw, Trumbo told him silently. He always made a big show of passing the time of day with the man, talking him up, but he did not really trust him—except to be glad of the extra few bucks every month from feeding the dogs. One time Trumbo had stopped by the door to talk to the man, who had run a little black-and-white TV out the door on an extension cord and set it on an upended concrete block. He was a bristly-looking old character, his rarely shaven chin like a piece of a worn-out nylon brush. He took the eternal toothpick out of his lower lip and spit a black stream that stretched out all the way to the ground for several seconds.

"Heard a feller," he offered, "say them hybrids was liable to be wild."

The usual attitude of those people about anything not their own, Trumbo thought, which was to say practically everything. "Mm. Wasn't the feller I heard," he tossed back, and by his manner let the man know he did not credit what he said.

Oh, it bothered him a little bit. He knew those animals would never make watchdogs. When he drove up the rutted weed-grown road to the pen, they would recognize the rumble of the hot-rod truck and hurl themselves against the fence, but silently, except for the impact of their bodies, the sound of their claws striking wood. They wouldn't bark, just give a little woof and back off. But they did not seem wild, and after a few weeks they came when Trumbo whistled, whether they were tied to the ropes or not. They began to fill out too. Trumbo dropped by at odd hours to see that the old man actually gave them the good food he provided and did not mistreat them in any way. They were looking good.

And after the dogs would come when he whistled, he started teaching them to ride in the truck. In the dry scabby Texas autumn, the evenings shorter by then, he would give the command and hoist the dogs up into the truckbed one by one— and how light they were, all legs and tail and surprise at being in the air. Then he would tie them down, pulling the rope taut on the truckbed, and take off down towards the blacktop to drive a few miles at road speed. At first they seemed afraid, of the loud surface where they lay and the loud air rushing past. But they got used to it. In time, at the command alone they would jump up and sit or lie quietly in the back of the truck while he bumped back over the old man's excuse for a drive-way and out onto the road. In time, they did not seem to know whether they were tied down or not.

After they could ride in the truck, he started taking them out for runs in the hills: he could see they were built to run. Their ribs no longer showed by then, and they were coming into their winter coats, the long parti-colored hairs standing up in ruffs around their necks. He would drive out to some ungated dirt road off the blacktop and turn off and let them down out of the truck and off they would go, heads down and long-legged, snuffling, gazing, seeking the crests of hills and ridges, the high ground in the lowering afternoon sun. He would watch them go with a feeling of mingled triumph and fear. And then, before they had gone too far, he whistled. They stopped and raised their heads, and he was not sure, in that mo-ment—he believed, but was not sure—that they would obey, but he whistled again, and there they came a-running. And always he felt enormously gratified and justified at that, and at how, at his command, they jump-pulled themselves up into the back of the truck with a clumsy double motion.

Then he could think of his triumphs, of the good fortune and right decisions in his life, even going back to the Depres-sion Oklahoma of his childhood, where his real mother had given him to her sister when he was three days old, so that he grew up calling his real mother "Aunt" and his aunt "Mother" in what he had known early on was the first good trade of his life. Watching the children his real mother and father had kept, both older and younger, traipse by on the dusty road, he had recognized them for a shiftless lot. At seventeen he had gone to California with ten dollars his aunt gave him in his shoe. Or he could recall the time in the fifties when he owned a small chain of three dry-cleaning stores and did not seem to be getting anywhere and learned to fly lightplanes and worked as a pilot three days a week in Nevada and bought rent houses with the money, which had proved to be the foundation for everything he did later.

And every time he took those dogs out like that, he knew they might not come back—in an obscure way, that was why he did it—but every time, they did. Then one day, on the way back to the pen, he thought of a little piece of hardware he needed that he could get from Sears. Somebody had dented the truck for him, backed into it in a parking lot, and he meant to fix it, which he could do practically with scarred, hard hands alone—long ago, he had owned a body shop in L.A. But he needed just one thing. The dogs would wait quietly in the truck, he thought, no problem. And when he glanced back at them from across the parking lot at the mall, they were sitting up in the back of the truck like pie and ice cream, only not smiling; he had noticed they were different in this way from other dogs. Then the automatic door sighed open to let him in.

But he had no more passed under the goose, a big papier-mâché goose hanging from the ceiling of the mall two stories up—because this was just a few weeks before Christmas—when he heard people behind him saying ". . . dogs in here!" and knew at once both that they couldn't be his and that they were. There they came, toenails clicking on the polished stone floor. You'd've thought—he thought, but they *were* in, and then he thought they would come to him when he whistled, but they ran on past through the crowd with just a little flick of the ear, seemed to say, shaft you, buddy.

But then he thought he'd catch them, inside as they were, box them up someplace and get ahold of them, so he followed them, moving as fast as he could without making it positively clear they were his. That proved an excellent precaution. Because then they ran into a store and snatched at a red fox jacket, which pulled over the rack the thing was chained to and set off the inventory control beeper, and then the grand foofaraw was on. They tore through the sidewalk cafe, scattering signs and chairs and customers. They ran through the papier-mâché floor display, knocking over a cardboard Bambi, a Christmas party of smaller animals, and a small paper tree. This nearly tripped a pregnant woman who was pushing a stroller full of packages, at which point Trumbo knew he was in a mess of trouble if anybody found out those dogs were his.

Then he had the brilliant idea that maybe they would run right through the shopping center and come out the other side, that all he had to do was move the truck around there, and they'd just run out and jump in it and he could drive away with them. In the stress of the moment, this seemed like such a wonderful solution to him that he could see it happening, could see it happening so clearly that then he couldn't see it *not* happening. So he went back out to the truck in a fever of hope and confidence and moved it around to the other side of the mall, but as he began to know by the time he got there, this tactic was futile.

Sitting there in the yellow El Camino, his body revving on adrenaline, he had a vision of what if they did come, trailing a long string of the irate and injured. He'd be sued hairless, he thought. He got to worrying that somebody had seen those dogs jump out of the truck to begin with and would remember—it was so distinctive. So he drove off without them, looking back and back again for them as he went, still by force of will believing every time that he'd see them, running out to jump in the truck, but he never did. He never saw them again, and he never knew what happened to them.

When he pulled out onto the highway and began to power up the hill, it kept on rising ahead of him. There seemed to be something moving in the world, heaving under him, like a giant creature waking up.

The World Record Holder

Balancing on One Foot. The longest recorded duration for continuously balancing on one foot without any rests is 35 hours by Mary Eileen Maloney, Wichita Falls, Texas, on March 3, 198–. The disengaged foot may not be rested on the standing foot nor may any sticks be used for support or balance.

198– World Book of Records

We've both changed—even from the beginning of our acquaintance, in the two sides of a duplex full of construction errors in blatant Ft. Worth, we were moving in opposite directions. I was married, wanting to be single, and she was single, wanting to be married, a thin rapid intelligent woman, christened Mary Eileen, called Emmy. She was sharing the other side of the duplex with another schoolteacher and a nurse, a tall clear-eyed blonde named Marilyn, and Marilyn was getting married. This had set Emmy's mind like a bright weather vane, gargoyle and arrow, at the same angle for days on end.

"I hate her," Emmy would say. "She's so happy. And she gets into the car with him"—it was an unshiny old red Ford convertible, Marilyn's, not his, but this was no help to Emmy—"and they drive off together, and I can't stand it, I'm so jealous, I want somebody to love me." And we would laugh, at the absurd persistence of ambition, or longing, or something.

It seems like a long time ago, now that I wake up alone so many different places later, with the light diffused through the curtains, the pyracantha outside, lacy or brilliant with the season. I'm simpler, easier now, like the birds: a cardinal flew into the room one time and almost miraculously made it out unbroken; another time a mockingbird flew against the window outside, cracking the pane, and was killed.

But when I met Emmy, who was a stranger in town, accidental, like my then-husband and me, she offered the kindness of distraction, a life even more difficult-seeming than my own. At home all day alone—the other schoolteacher did something

3 5

else in the summer, and Marilyn worked a day shift—Emmy
would wait for me to drive up and would rush out and leap
on me conversationally. She would invite me in, make me iced
tea for the shimmering Texas afternoon, and tell me all about
herself and everything she was thinking.

"I'm thirty-one!" she said. "Can you believe it? I hate my
job, my car is broken, my family is crazy, and I want a man!"

Crazy was one of her words, not as a casual comment but
as a serious assessment ("Of course, *I'm* crazy, *you're* crazy—
you must be or you wouldn't've married him—but he's *really*
crazy"). Also necessary credential ("I mean," she said, "if they
weren't crazy, why would we care about them?"), ambiguous
good ("But what I want to know," she said, "is just how crazy
a person can be and still walk around in the world?"), and gen-
erally significant topic of inquiry all around—what it meant
that you had to be crazy but not too crazy.

She was preoccupied, as well, with larger and larger questions ("I mean, what's it all *good* for?" she would say. "What's
it all *about*? I mean, okay, great, if you can be James Joyce, or
Picasso, or Duke Ellington, but what if you can't?"), so that
conversations with her were likely to end in a companionship
of exhaustion and irresolution on the outer margins of human
circumstance.

"I used to think about committing suicide," she said, "after I read Camus—silly, isn't it, kill yourself because of a
book?—but really, what's the good of even that? I mean, we're
just *here*."

And I could agree with her, for all the else I knew about it,
or know now, only for me it's more like a song we used to
sing in the Scouts: "Here we stand like birds in the wilder-
ness . . . Waiting to be fed." I never really shared her noble
desperation. I'm a gardener now. I seed and feed and cherish
new roots and shoots, and when I die, I'm going to be composted, and it's enough for me, or I make do.

But if I wasn't to have a future like hers, I didn't have such a
past either. She had an unusual family history: she was the

daughter of a jockey named Eddie Maloney, who had been famous once, when he rode a horse named War Department to win the Belmont Stake in 1930-something. He had been an Irish kid from Canada, an orphan, or maybe a runaway; he had grown up around racing and started riding races in New York in the early thirties.

And one time in New Orleans for the winter racing, her father had met her mother—he was in traction in the hospital, and she was a nurse. Later they sold their story to MGM—I saw it when I was a kid, years before I knew Emmy: at first he's the rough-tongued young jock, desperate over this setback to his career; then sweet-faced Jane Wyman, playing the good Catholic girl, nurses him back to health; and in the end War Department wins and it's all going to be so perfect.

I wonder, did they ever see the movie? He would've, a devotee of his own myth; she would've been working the evening shift at some hospital so she could get the kids off to school in the morning. He had made money and spent it like all the jocks, on custom-made suits and a silver fox topcoat and a 1936 Cord 810 and a claque of friends. Because, of course, he thought it would go on and on, that he had well and truly made it, and he almost became what they call a legendary figure in racing. Was it drinking? They all drank. Maybe it wasn't anything he did or didn't do. Somehow, in the gradual algebra of opinion that meant you got the winning mounts, he didn't anymore, though he had continued to ride; it was what he knew how to do.

"The last year my father raced," Emmy said—I think it was 1950—"he rode eighty races and made altogether less than two thousand dollars."

So he retired from racing and moved the family to New Orleans, which had been the mother's home.

"I'm from nowhere," Emmy said. "One time we lived in a trailer. When I was sixteen, I became the Yankee kid. I think that's what I like about the South."

"In the house we lived in," she said, "you could see the

fairgrounds race track from one upstairs window and the St. Louis Number Three Cemetery from the other one. Now they live on Mystery Street."

Her father still did things around the track—"Oh, he drinks," Emmy said. "He hangs out with his racing buddies and they talk"—and her mother was still a nurse. She worked at the emergency room of a hospital in New Orleans called the Hôtel Dieux.

A little poorer year by year as the children were growing up, they had sent Emmy's younger brother to college, but not Emmy—she'd had to work her way through.

"So here I am with a lousy degree from a lousy university," she said, "so I can't get into a really good graduate school, like Harvard or Yale, or Berkeley or Columbia—though those places are sort of crazy right now—I mean, the list of places I can't get into is positively depressing. So what can I do? Teach high school in Grapevine, Texas, and waste away to nothing." She had taken the job in Texas sight unseen, for the strangeness of it ("I mean, Grapevine!" she said), as if her personal supply of improbability wouldn't've been enough.

She had freckles on her arms that ran together in places and a head of spiky blond hair that she bleached some and cut herself, short, like on Giulietta Masina playing the idiot girl in *La Strada*. At one time in life she had wanted to travel, and she had been to Europe and the Middle East and had once taught in a private girls' school in Iran for a year and caught typhoid and lost all her hair, but it had grown back.

"I was kind of sorry," she said. "Think if I was bald. At least that would be *something*."

It wasn't enough, I suppose, that she looked like her father, or maybe it was too much. I met him once: he looked like Charlie McCarthy, only about four-feet-eleven, with skin like wood and a narrow, angular little body like a Chinese woman's foot, when they used to do that, or a crippled child.

They had driven up from New Orleans for a visit, and I had

been invited over to meet them, to water down this family combination the exact asperity of which I could never truly share, and we were standing in Emmy's avocado kitchen, where there were gaps around the all-electric appliances.

"Say," Eddie said to me, "I bet you didn't get up as early this morning as I did." He was drinking Canadian Club poured out of a bottle he had brought with him into a cloudy Flintstones glass his daughter had undoubtedly had to wash for him.

"You have to get up early to be a jockey," he said, and looked up from under white eyebrows with the calculated timing of a man who makes jokes for a living or as a regular mode of conversation. "It's a profession, you might say, singularly unforgiving of lateness."

I was the only one who laughed, and he went on smoothly, "There was once a jock at our track"—as if he had already linked all his stock of remarks and stories in all possible combinations, so that none could be difficult or unfamiliar— "name of George Woolf, a diabetic, by the way, who fell asleep one morning in a turkish bath trying to sweat off a couple of pounds for the weigh-in and missed the mount of the summer meet."

He had on a suit in the cut of the forties, neither new nor worn-looking, clean and pressed, with an air of the closet about it, and expensive-looking wing tips laced tight on insignificant bunioned feet. He saw me looking at them.

"I had the right feet for a jock. That was how they knew I wouldn't grow."

Emmy had taken a Librium for the visit and smoked Salems one after another. She seemed divided: should she show him off, the once-famous jockey father who told stories—he was, after all, what she had—or was he really, as he had seemed to her in the family for years, a terrible bore?

"Oh, Poppy," she said. Her mother was a tall cool brunette, still a beauty in her fifties, with a perfect mask, the discipline, maybe, of thirty years' listening.

"Get up early and stay late," he said. "There was another rider—steeplechase rider—name of Hayes, rode a horse name of Sweet Kiss home first in Belmont Park and fell out of the saddle dead.

"Now that's dedication for you."

Eventually we changed the subject, while Eddie's memories ran on silently under him, like the horses of the past. Finishing his drink, reaching to pour another, he shook his head and smiled out of one corner of his stiff mouth.

"Like asking a Cadillac for mercy," he said, as if to himself, without rancor.

We moved away after the summer—we didn't live in that house but a few months—and spent the last thin year of the marriage in Atlanta, Georgia, where getting divorced turned out to be vastly and surprisingly simple. Emmy and I wrote letters about how strangely simple it was and about other things, she, long inchoate letters that seemed to have gone on like her conversations, until she was exhausted. Our friendship settled into a long-distance pattern not so different from the way it had been when we lived next door to each other, except there was no iced tea. The next year she did go to graduate school, though not to any of the places on the list of places she couldn't get into. Then she wrote me about "how *crazy* this place is" and how much she was in love with one of her professors, who was married, and what a shit he was, but she got over him.

Then she wrote, as a postscript to some other circling self-examination, "There's this man, this man. I don't know."

Months later, there he still was, having moved in, or rather, she wrote, come over one night and never left, introducing his things, a clean shirt, a pair of forgotten underdrawers, one at a time.

"We share our disillusion," she wrote. "We laugh a lot and he's a great big warm bear. He's younger than me—eleven

years, can you believe it?" But it was a surprise when they
decided one weekend and got married the next, in New Orleans at the registry office.

"Unbelievable," she wrote, "that I can be this happy, though,
of course, the wedding itself was ridiculous."

She sent me a Polaroid taken indoors, the color too yellow,
of herself, her tiny waist in a blue-and-white polka-dotted wrap
dress, holding a plastic champagne glass and laughing, next to
a large, reassuring-looking young man with brown eyes and a
large brown beard.

"Of course, my father was drunk, and the rest of the family—
my brother, my mother's cousins, who don't like my father—
were just standing around. And none of Doyle's family came
down from Texas, though we invited them, not even his
mother. They're like that."

After this, unsurprisingly, she wrote less often and less when
she wrote, as if her conversational energy were being spent
elsewhere. And when she did write, it was not about what it
was like to've gotten what she wanted but about the medium-
sized details of their life. Graduate school, which neither of
them liked much. "If you could just read great literature," she
wrote, but there was so much other bullshit, but on the other
hand, it was an education ("Why do we think that's good?" she
wrote. "Maybe it's just another shibboleth. Or are doubts
about the value of education becoming themselves a new shibboleth? What a word").

Then, before they had been married a year, Doyle was about
to be drafted. "He tried to flunk the physical," she wrote
"—his blood pressure is naturally high—staying up all night
the night before, taking dexies and drinking Coca-Cola and
telling me to shout at him, so I screamed and screamed, but
when he went in, it was just under."

It all worked out, though, since they could be saved by moving to Doyle's hometown so he could take a public service job
there. "They don't really *need* any more bodies from Wichita

Falls," she wrote. "Volunteering is popular there." So they quit graduate school, gratefully, it seemed, and moved to Wichita Falls, where Doyle got a job with Child and Family Services ("I never knew they *had* that there," she wrote), and they bought a house and were having a baby.

Only then was she disposed to reflect on what she had achieved. "I never thought I'd do this," she wrote, "sit home all day in my own little house in my own little town (actually, it's Doyle's little town). I even cook, sort of—remember Ft. Worth, with the books on the oven shelf? And it's fine, it's perfectly all right."

And I thought perhaps it was true, perhaps I was only unconvinced because my own experience had been different, though she did still seem afflicted with a certain nervous, half-resentful distance from her life. But that might just have been the burden of a naturally ironic outlook.

After the baby was born, she wrote, "I look at her, and I'm supposed to feel something. What is this word *motherhood* that I'm supposed to feel?"

And when Melissa was a couple of years old, Emmy wrote, "I look at her when she's decided she *won't* do something, and I think, who are you? You're not my child. You're not *mine*. Of course, she looks *exactly* like me."

It was around this time that, back in Ft. Worth, I went up to see them, to flat Wichita Falls. We sat around in their little white frame house in their grown-up living room, which had carpeting and drapes and a green plaid Early American sofa and some maple tables covered with glass that all seemed to've been bought secondhand at the same time and put there and not thought about since. But Emmy and Doyle were happy; they said so, and they looked happy. They were standing together in front of the cold fireplace facing me, Emmy with her head tucked under Doyle's chin.

I said, "You're the only people I know for whom marriage has actually seemed to make life better."

"Oh, it has," she said.

"We are too," he said, "the only people we know." And I thought, yes, it must happen sometimes. I liked Doyle; he was easygoing, noncommittal, humorous; she seemed to've made a stabilizing choice.

On another visit, though, months later, I was less convinced. Things seemed less blissful, more familiar somehow, as if an earlier reality of Emmy's life had reasserted itself. "I just vegetate," she said. "I don't have any friends. I've turned into a *lump*. I try to write and can't. Then I sit down and drink gin every day. Or I go out to the thrift shop and buy, ugly things to cheer myself up, just because they're two-fifty, and I come home and look at them and wonder what I bought *that* for, and Doyle makes fun of me."

They'd been married about four years then. She laughed about their sex life. "He used to wake me *up* at six o'clock in the morning. I couldn't believe it. I'm a *rag* at six A.M., a *rag*."

But none of this seemed serious, or any worse than the known blunt ordinary of marriage, so I didn't doubt that they would make out, laugh at her discontent together, do something sensible about it.

Instead, they decided to have another baby. Emmy wrote, "I'm a nervous wreck. Doyle made me give up smoking this time. I can't even drink, because it nauseates me. All I do is sleep. I fall asleep in the middle of meals, like the dormouse, or I'll just be sitting there."

But when the baby was born, she wrote, "This is my child. I look at Adam and I just love him. Melissa is so jealous—no wonder, I never felt this way about her."

And then, passing through Dallas–Ft. Worth on another one of those crossings of the South that seem to've been part of my affliction at the time, I ran up on short notice for a weekend visit and into their own misery, without knowing.

In the back yard, the grass was brown and dry and the ground as hard as fired clay, and Emmy and Doyle, standing apart from me, went on with some discussion they had started before I got there. I was pushing Melissa on the swing and didn't hear, but Emmy was earnest, gesturing with her arms, saying most of the words, while Doyle was looking, as if absentmindedly, away.

Privately, with Adam asleep in the bassinet in the dining room, Emmy worried to me. "I'm going to waste. I try to write, but I can't. We have crazy friends. We see this couple, Doyle's social work professor at Midwestern." Doyle was having to get credits towards an M.S.W. to get promoted in his job. "I think both of us are in love with him. Last time they came over, all four of us ending up shouting at each other. I can't stand this guy. He intimidates me so—you should see the way Doyle and him exclude me."

And hearing it all again, I didn't feel as sympathetic as I had. I thought maybe her capacity for dissatisfaction was constant, and only its objects would change.

She did have a friend of her own by then, which I thought might help her, a locally well-known landscape painter—we went to see some of her vapory watercolors in the lobby of a famous old hotel—but the woman herself I didn't like much.

"Sylvia's crazy, too," Emmy said. "She threw her husband out, but they're still married. He comes around in his pickup truck begging her to let him move back into the house. It's embarrassing." He was a toolpusher in the oilfield. Sylvia hadn't known how to tell him she wanted a divorce, so she had the papers served on him as a way of bringing up the subject. One Sunday morning they were in the bathtub fooling around, and he got out of the tub to answer the door, and there it was: his wife wanted a divorce.

I had arrived complaining about money, worrying whether I had enough for the cross-country move I was in the middle of, doubting even whether I should've spent the money to come to Wichita Falls. Seeing me off on Sunday night, cordial as always, Doyle stuffed a twenty-dollar bill into my hand. "Anyway, it'll cover your bus ticket," he said, and though I tried to give it back, he wouldn't take it, saying, "Keep it, keep it. I can afford it more than you."

I tried to give it to Emmy, who I thought would've taken it, but instead she just laughed. "Oh, you have to indulge him. He gives people canned goods when they come over. They say something like, 'We have to go shopping, there's absolutely nothing to eat in the house,' and he gives them a can of tuna-fish to take with them."

Years later, Emmy confessed to me in a letter that after I left that time there had been a terrible fight about money. "When was the last time you gave me twenty dollars?" she screamed at him. "When did you *ever* just *give* me twenty dollars be-cause you had it and I didn't?" But for months after that visit, we hardly wrote, maybe not even friends anymore.

Then, in a couple of years, it was all over: they were break-ing up, and who could really say why?

"It's horrible," she wrote after a long time, as if diverted by desperation into letters again. "Doyle is being horrible. He's a stone. He disappears behind the newspaper. He sleeps on the sofa. I say, 'Do you love me?' and he says nothing. I drink and take pills. My shrink says I have low self-esteem and I demand too much of myself, but I ask you, what do I do that I should hold in esteem? I hate my daughter, love my son madly, no longer even try to write, and drink gin in the afternoons. Then my husband comes home and won't talk to me. Once he didn't say a single word, I swear, not one single word, for two solid weeks. I would sit on the arm of the chair where he was read-ing the paper and *scream* at him, 'I'm here. Talk to me,' and he'd never move a muscle."

I wrote back, advice she couldn't follow, probably, and we were friends again in disaster, another marriage in trouble. I felt sorry for Doyle and thought she might have been kinder to him, but it was clear that she couldn't be, and though I liked him and didn't blame him the way she did, she was my friend, not he. I remember the very moment when, reading some letter of hers, I knew and regretted I'd never see him again. The marriage lasted altogether about eight years.

She wrote, "It's over. It's completely and forever over, though we're still living in the house together until he can afford to move out. One night in December after he came home, I don't know why I did this, I went into the bedroom and looked in his coat pocket and found this expensive turquoise necklace, much nicer than anything he ever bought me. So I went downstairs and said, 'Do you love me?' and he said, 'No,' and that was that. I never told him I found the necklace.

"And I know—I'm so crazy—I know they're going to take my kids away from me, and I can't stand the thought, can't stand the *idea* of Doyle trying to raise them, Doyle the stone. As crazy as I am, I *know* I'm a better parent than he is, but I can't *stand*, either, the idea of having to go in and try to convince somebody I'm sane."

She did it, though, surprising herself if not me. "After *seventeen*—would you believe it?—seventeen sessions of psychiatric evaluation," she wrote, "I've got the kids. Doyle brought out all this *horrible* stuff in court—my diary, for God's sake, that I've been keeping off and on since I was twenty. I mean, what do you *do* when you're home all day with nobody to talk to? Only, it's all, you know, not what's really happening. I mean, in my life I'm getting the kids up and fixing breakfast for everybody and getting Melissa off to school and doing the laundry and cleaning up where the cat was sick and going out to the Safeway for two cans of tomato sauce and a package of Rice-a-Roni, but of course none of that's in the diary. What's in the *diary* is how crazy and miserable I am, how I'm losing my mind, and how much Valium I'm taking. That was the other big exhibit, my Valium prescriptions."

"So now it's over, and I have the children, and Doyle the stone is living in an apartment and seeing some woman—not the same one, I think—and I have collapsed in total relief."

And that was the apparent end of the ambition I'd first known her with.

She wrote, "I feel totally empty, exhausted." Her friend Sylvia had painted a picture called something like "Out of Luck in the Oilfield" that I remembered, a man in an aluminum hard hat, a human line of despair against the angle of the derrick, the impervious expanse of prairie behind.

Afterwards, she was just holding on, just maintaining herself and the children. She got a job at the last minute, right before school started in September.

"They want me to teach something called Multi-Media Communication, about which I know nothing. What it is, really, is non-college-prep required English. Can you imagine that? Teaching semiliterate high school students about television and popular music, when what's *wrong* with them is all they've done all their lives is watch television and listen to popular music?"

By spring, she was writing, "I dread going to work. I hate my students, and they hate me. It's so absurd. Every day we all—most of us, anyway—force ourselves to go to this place where we don't want to be, and we hate every minute that we're there—and in this atmosphere somebody is supposed to *learn* something? What a joke."

She struggled to take care of the children. "And then, every afternoon I drag myself home, pick up the kids from *two separate* day-care centers (in one of which they are turning my son into a Baptist!), and then I try to make dinner. Tonight we had peanut butter and jelly, because I was too tired even to make Kraft Dinner. And now I'm supposed to grade papers!"

Doyle did pay child support. "Big deal!" she wrote. "If anybody had ever told me I would be supporting two children on the amount of money I am, and that it would buy this little, I wouldn't've believed them."

By the end of the school year she wrote, "I am never going to enter a classroom again. I will do anything else."

And she must've looked for jobs, and it must've been that, with everything else, that overwhelmed her, but she didn't write me about it. She waited till I was there, the next summer, a year later, to tell me. In Dallas for something, I had taken the bus up to spend an evening with her, and we were sitting out in the back yard on aluminum lawn chairs on the unwatered grass, watching five-year-old Adam play soberly by himself.

"It's been hard for me to accept that he's a very ordinary child," she said. "In fact, he's slow-average. When he was born, I thought . . . oh, everything." She laughed.

Melissa was nine, freckled, strawberry blond, somehow appearing only around the edges of any scene. She did look like Emmy, and like Eddie Maloney, but with a baleful aplomb that made her seem more like Doyle. I hoped it would help her.

Emmy said, "I, ha-ha, did a very foolish thing. I had quit teaching forever, after that awful year, and I couldn't find a job, and I decided that I just couldn't struggle anymore. I mean, I was so tired, and I had hardly any money left, and there was going to be a nuclear war anyway, and Wichita Falls would get it because of the Air Force base, so I decided to kill the children and myself. I went out to buy a gun. I had this whole elaborate story cooked up to tell them about why I wanted it, in case they were suspicious. And you know what? The cheapest one you could get—l think it was eighty-nine ninety-five—was more money than I had in the world. I couldn't afford to kill myself."

Instead she had found a job "working for a bunch of psychologists," she had written at the time. "It might be a sort of secretary-editorial job." But by the time I saw her, months later, she knew, "all I'll ever be there is a secretary. What I do all day is fill out forms on the typewriter just as fast as I can, with these guys standing over me telling me to hurry up. I walk out of there at night *shaking*, I'm not kidding."

It was better than teaching, though, "if I *do* have to go to work in July," she said. "At least when I get off, I'm *off*—no essays to read. And these guys (these guys are so weird), at least they're grown-ups and they don't tell you to get fucked."

There were men in her life again, but they were indistinct, rising to the surface of her conversation only to be glimpsed now and then ("Oh, *Mike*," she said. "Mike always wanted to go to *bed*. I wanted to go to the *movies* or something"). She didn't seem positively to care about anything except performing the motions of household and family life, and I wondered if she would always be this way now, like a stuffed hawk in the children's museum, legs outthrust towards something that had gotten away a long time before.

Six months or so later, the Christmas letter, probably, she wrote that her father had died of a heart attack and her mother had intestinal cancer, a diagnosis which, oddly for a nurse, she rejected until the end, which came quickly. And partly, it seemed, under the influence of grief, Emmy left the psychologists' job ("I couldn't stand it after a while—all that fake *understanding* going around, when none of those people really gives a shit about me," she wrote), and in one of those curious generational patterns that beset our lives, worked briefly as a clerk in the emergency ward of a hospital. She also went back into psychotherapy, where she was prescribed lithium, which she thought changed things for her ("I'm so *calm*," she wrote. "What have I become? Hopelessly and unutterably boring, and you know what? I don't *care*. My kids even like me better, I don't *yell* at them like I used to.").

In the fall, she took her new calmness back to teaching. "It's the only halfway interesting job I have any qualifications for. Plus, the bottom tracks seem a little more cowed here. I can make them sit there and shut up and *read*—even if the only

thing some of them can read is comic books. And I am *calm*,
whatever they do, it doesn't get my goat. I'm not even sure I
still have a goat.

"I don't do much else. I come home from teaching and I'm
tired. Still, I tell myself, I'm doing something. I'm supporting
myself and my children, and it's *hard*.

"When I have the strength, though, I sometimes wonder, is
this all there is?"

Around this time—encouragingly, I thought—she began
looking for whatever else there might be. Possibly under advice from her psychiatrist ("None of my gym teachers would
believe this," she wrote), she took up running. ("I go out after
work and pound around the track like one of my father's two-
year-olds, in a little red shiny outfit that I got from the secondhand shop, shorts and a tank top, with a white stripe, and wonder if my children are anything like psychologically normal.")
It did not satisfy her, and she wrote, "You should see me. I
have to stop this before I disappear. I weigh 91 pounds. And
it's so boring, so *boring*, so *boring*, it has no *soul*, no *meaning*.
Is that what makes it good? That it's like life? I don't need this
for recreation."

But she needed something, for something, and at this time
in her life the physical seemed to compel her, so she switched
to Jazzercise. She wrote, "I go to Adult Ed twice a week. It's
silly, of course, paying somebody fifty dollars to stand up there
and show you how to 'work your body.' When I first heard
that, I thought it was 'walk your body,' like a dog. Christ, listening to that mindless music, sometimes I think I'll—but then
the endorphines or whatever they are hit and I don't care. I
feel good. (Is that what life is all about? Just feeling good?)

"Of course, a lot of these people have religion. It's popular
again everywhere now, isn't it, and especially down here. But
I went to Catholic schools and I got out of that once and for
all. I mean, where do they get off? Telling people that God

hasn't actually *spoken* to anybody except a few cracked saints for centuries and centuries, but we know he's still up there, and moreoever *we* know what he wants *you* to do!"

In the end, though, or I wouldn't be writing this, she did find what she was looking for, or something that would do. Like the whooping cranes that winter down on the coast here and fly up the Great Plains to Canada every spring—they prefer a certain kind of wild tubers, I understand, but in a sparse year, they make do with water rats, insects, aquatic life. After all, they're almost extinct.

It had been months since I heard from her, and she wrote, "You won't believe this, but I am, as they say, 'into' standing around on one foot. And I thought awhile, after I wrote that. What kind of thing is that to write to a friend after six months? (Is this my semiannual letter to you?) It's true, though. It started when my friend Marty—did I tell you about Marty?—was over and we were drunk and reading *The Guinness Book of Records*, and I read there that somebody in Sri Lanka had set the world record for standing on one foot, and it's 33 hours. And I thought, I can do that. I mean, I've been doing it all my life in one way or another. It fits my temperament: it's difficult but not too difficult, demanding in a sort of simple way but not too demanding, and it's a chance to set a world record, right down there in black and white!

"Is it worth doing? Of course not, not compared to being Shakespeare (but Shakespeare didn't really *know* he was Shakespeare, did he? I mean, that four hundred years later to people in the English-speaking world, he'd still be *Shakespeare*? So what good was it to him?). Anyhow, I'm not Shakespeare, I'm 46 years old (can you believe it? I'm old! and I haven't even grown up yet), and the world will probably be blown up in my lifetime, and being in the book of world records for standing on one foot is *something*.

"The first time I tried it, I fainted and fell over after 6 hours.

Everything went black. I was standing in the middle of the living room carpet. I was lucky I didn't hit my head on the hearth or something, I could've been killed. Instead, I fell on a table and broke my arm. Fortunately, I could train with a broken arm—in fact, I couldn't do much else. I think if I'd quit right then I never would've tried it again. Maybe I kept on *because* I broke my arm. Now I'm up to 13 hours and there's no doubt in my mind that I can do it eventually—unless I get varicose veins or cancer or something."

And that was how she came to it, by what might be called chance. Any doubts I might've raised, she had raised herself and disposed of already, so (myself raking and piling up in one season, strewing and scattering in another) I wrote to her soothing, favorable things, a selection of the best you can write to an old friend newly standing competitively on one foot.

She kept me up on her progress: "I'm up to 19 hours. I work out while I read high school students' essays. I used to hold them in my hands, but that was messing up my stance, so now I leave them on the mantelpiece and just turn the pages. And I make jokes about it—that at least I have a leg to stand on, or that I have a leg up, or that I'm going to lift a leg (you're allowed hourly pee breaks)."

Towards the end she wrote, "It's hard to find time to test endurance and still get everything done. I've given up sleeping on Saturday nights. I'm up to 26 hours, free stand on one foot. My friend Lola comes in and helps out (Did you know that people here will just help you sometimes, because you ask them to? I never knew that).

"I drink green Kool-Aid and nibble on something. The children feed themselves, and they know they can come and talk to me but I cannot come and take care of anything unless they need to go to the hospital. (Did I write you about the time I did have to take Adam? He fell down the back steps and broke his ankle. Do you think that was so he could only stand on one foot too? He was calling me from out there, saying, 'Mommy, I can't stand up,' and I was saying, 'Adam, you better be really hurt, or I am going to be very angry with you.' He was in a cast for a month. Eight-year-olds heal fast.)

"I'm not going to overtrain. When I can almost do it, I'm going to set up the verification procedures and go for it. Listen to me, 'go for it.' Have I simply found a way to be the same kind of idiot everybody else is?"

The rest appears in the public annals of unusual achievement. "On March 2–3," she wrote, "a day of local historical interest, for whatever it's worth. And I wasn't, I honestly wasn't sure I was going to make it from hour 30 to hour 33. But then I thought, why not go on and on? And I believed I could. Marty says I was hallucinating mildly by then. So I did it, and it's been accepted by the *Book* and will come out, I don't know when.

"It's absurd, isn't it? But what isn't, anymore? There's a certain letdown afterwards. So I did it, so what? What now? I suppose there's always terminal boredom; I've had a lot of experience with that. It's not easy coming to terms with your own mediocrity."

No. At first I'd planned to be composted and fed to roses— I've always loved roses—it was in my will that way, but now I've decided to change it to a simpler flower, a native flower. Bitterweed? Bull-nettle, a surprisingly beautiful blossom? Day-flower? That was in another codicil, but now I'm thinking fire-wheel. I'll be composted and fed to fire-wheels, along the never-plowed right-of-way, where the native grasses still seed.

Now Emmy writes, "I'm keeping in training. Every day I come home from work and stand on one foot for several hours. I mean, sometime the record is bound to be challenged—maybe even by the man in Sri Lanka next year."

I have plans to go up for a visit soon. I feel concerned about her daughter, somehow, who's eleven, almost a young woman herself, with who knows what ambitions? Emmy writes, "Melissa has gotten to be a very good cook. She makes things out of *The Joy of Cooking* and other books that people gave me—you know, the ones I always used to look at and think I *could* make something out of there, but instead would make something out of a package? She even seems to enjoy it, though it's hard to tell with Melissa."

Like Family

When Dinny first saw Thomas, in the honky-tonk down the beach where she takes the children sometimes for lunch, she had a feeling about him right away. He was standing at the bar hunched over a glass of beer, like he didn't have the price of another one. At that time she was already thinking about having versus not having money. He was little and dark and taut, with his hair hanked back in a thick ponytail on his neck. Søren, her youngest, went right up to him. So she knew, she told people solemnly afterwards, that he was all right: "Children can tell." He played with the children, feint and fence, springing up on booted feet like an elf.

Then their hamburgers came, frilled with bright green leaves of lettuce, and he told Søren, "Go eat your food," and turned away, and that, too, was a plus.

They were rich, Thomas could see, or had money around them—not by their faded shorts and shirts at the beach or the old blue VW squareback they had driven up in but by more permanent things: skin, teeth, the straight-backed confidence of the four blond boys, even the athletic frumpiness of the woman. Also, they were a real family. Being in a manner of speaking an orphan himself, he could see that. There was a father and husband somewhere nearby.

So when they had finished eating and the woman caught his eye and beckoned him to sit down at their table, he did, shyly, honored. He explained that he did not like to be called Tom. He showed her the briefcase he had made. It was dark brown leather, decorated with a three-color dyed design out of a Masonic book, a pyramid with eyes.

And as soon as Dinny saw that, she said afterwards, she knew he was one of hers, before she knew for what or why. Her father and all her brothers are Masons.

She gave the children quarters for video games so she could ask him about himself. He told her he grew up in orphanage, reform school, and jail, though he had not been back since he turned twenty-one. He was thirty years old and a leather craftsman.

"I don't need to be a thief," he said. "I can do it right."

A large woman, softly challenging, she wanted to know: "What did you steal?" When she speaks, she barely moves her large white face.

He remembered a radio, a strange pair of scissors he didn't know until he was picked up with them were called pruning shears.

Under the shadow bars that fell in on both of them from the big divided window, Dinny asked him, "But why?" His eyes were so black they did not seem to have any pupils.

"Beats me," he said. "It's no life. They get you in the end. Or you go crazy looking over your shoulder." The muscles of his sallow face came alive with thought, and he said, "But I 'member, looking at old houses, there was a certain kind of big old house."

She thought of their house, of her parents' house.

"Or businesses," he said. With his boy's hairless hand he stroked his handlebar mustache, which looked too big for him. "It was businesses with real good burglar alarms, only you'd look at them, and there'd be something, maybe just one thing wrong with it, that you could see, man, from the outside, how you could do it, easy as anything. I wanted to get in. And everytime when I did, I'd be so excited I'd have to find the john and go pee."

She deliberated, as if referring all of this to some entirely private standard.

Later, rounding up the children, Dinny invited him out to the house. "Come any time," she said in her airy way: somebody was always home.

And afterwards, at home, sitting at the white enamel kitchen table where she works out the problems of her family and other people, she thought about Thomas. She dealt the tarot for him: it came up the page of cups, which satisfied her.

She had told him her husband was an actor, and Thomas wondered what *he* would think, but went after a few days anyway. Borrowed a car from friends in the city and drove out to the island again: across the rumbling causeway where the water shines like metal chips; past the old hotels and the new condos; out to where the wind bends the bearded sea oats with nothing to stop it, and the hurricane washed right across.

There amid the dunes, like a great tattered ship at sea, rose the house. Later Thomas heard how Duff had spent all his inheritance (must be nice) to buy it when he and Dinny got married, and how it had been built in the thirties by a former governor of the state for his retirement, which was, however, disturbed by prosecutions for bribery and blackmail. But that first time, there was only the house, calling to Thomas, come in (-vited!). He went barreling up their sandy chute of a driveway.

And there *she* was, sitting at the window. He parked on the beach plum by a widening sink of sand and leaped from plank to scattered plank. They had new back steps, the lumber still unpainted. Without knocking, he went in the rusty screen door.

Pigtails jutted over her shoulders like gun barrels. "Hi, Shrimp," she said—she might've been his sister, if he'd had one.

"Hey, Dummy," he said, and this became the way they talked to each other. The kitchen was a mess, dishes rotting everywhere, laundry falling off chairs.

She was casting the *I Ching* to find out whether Werther should be held back in the third grade.

Duff was a voice in the house, the orotund tones of an actor filling some room beyond. Then he came in, wearing torn pajama bottoms, with his soft tan belly hanging over. He greeted Thomas as if he had known him for a long time. He had that same look of money that the rest of them had.

Then the room filled up with blond boys, and in what became the routine of Thomas's visits, men and boys ran together like drops of water out of the house and down through the dunes towards the wide Gulf beach, which, Thomas said one time afterwards—though it was a public right-of-way of the state that raised him—had never seemed like even partly his before.

Like a child, Dinny thought, to be taken into a family—that was what he needed. Not to create one, like Duff. Thomas was the son of a brain-damaged man who as a boy had been run over by the only Model A in a small inland town, his skull crushed, and had gotten a platinum plate in his skull and an article about it in a medical journal. In his teens, this man had married, but the girl hadn't stayed, and six months after she left had been arrested for prostitution in Corpus Christi. She was still only sixteen, and pregnant with Thomas. She did not want the baby herself, and the state would not give him to her husband, though he always insisted Thomas was his son. In this way, Thomas had come into the care of the state.

Which had not, Dinny thought, done such a great job. The first day she met Thomas, in the bar, she had asked him, from the geometric design on the briefcase, whether he was good in math. He'd already told her he only went through the eighth grade.

He said, "Nah, I wasn't good at nothing. They'd say, s'pose you got you an apple, then you get you another one, and I'd say, where, where?"

There was a little pause. "But why?" she said. ("Some dippy broad I met at the beach," he called her tenderly one time. "Some rich oil lawyer's daughter.")

He said, "Because I wanted to eat them, Dummy."

So the first time he came out there, she tried to feed him, pork chops and vegetables, just what they were having. He ate it all politely, then politely excused himself and went into the bathroom and threw up. He turned on the water to hide the sound, but she could tell. Later she found out the only

things Thomas liked to eat were bread and milk and mashed
potatoes.

The only thing that could help him by then was money.

"Not a shop!" he said scornfully, sitting at the kitchen table
with her one time, watching out the window for Duff and the
children to come back. "A factory!"

On the tabletop sat coffee cups with brown discs dried in
the bottoms, used plates with crusts and crumbs on them. Her
sloppiness irritated him: it seemed mental as well as physical.

He'd had a shop one summer on the mainland, with all the
rest of the craftfolks and not enough money he made dealing
lids. "And you bust your butt all day every day with nobody to
help you, and in the end you can't pay your rent."

Clueless, Thomas thought. She liked to call herself a white
witch; he told her to her face it was a crock.

"You got to join the twentieth century," he instructed her.
"Get a die! Stamp out your patterns! Hire a buncha Mexican
women to sit out in some warehouse and sew up belts and
bags. Sell quantity!"

One time she had laid conjure on their septic system because, she said, they could not afford to have it fixed. Later
there was a big hole in the sand half full of water where the
tank had to be dug up.

And yet as soon as he began telling her he knew she might
really help him. He had the feeling about her—had maybe
from the first time he talked to her—that she would do whatever she set out to. One way or another. It scared him a
little.

Then Duff, like a farmer amid a flock of chickens, turned
into sight with the children at the end of the driveway, and
Thomas was up and away, towards them.

"I love those people," Thomas said. "Those people are like
family to me."

"Duff has affairs," a theatrical acquaintance joked one time. "Dinny has projects." Getting the money for Thomas to go into business with became Dinny's project.

"Don't you think he should have it?" she asked Duff. "Don't you think he deserves it?"

Duff supposed so, cautiously. There was no telling what Dinny might do. Laughing, she said, "I could rob a bank," and he believed she meant it, but fortunately she realized she couldn't do it without Thomas's finding out, and Thomas would not've stood for it. (One time when they were in the supermarket and she didn't have enough money in her purse and was going to steal a can of tuna fish, Thomas threatened to walk home. "*You* do what *you* want to," he said, "but if you do *that*, I'm not with you.")

To the voodoo altar in the living room she added a picture of St. Raymond, who was good for money; there was already a picture of St. Anthony of Padua, who was good for love. She sprinkled something out of a bottle labeled "Fast Luck Water" and lit large candles, yellow for gold, green for money, that burned for nine days. It did not appear to Duff that anything happened, but as Dinny said, you never could tell. He had been married to her long enough to believe that.

"Sometimes I think I can almost think it," she said to him. "I mean, if I just think money, it will appear." So she sat there, apparently thinking money as hard as she could, but it didn't appear.

She took an egg, coated one side of it with mercury, and marked the ends of it like a compass, *N* and *S*, so it could find its way. Kneeling in the sand on her big white knees in the light that fell out of the kitchen window, she buried it at eleven o'clock one night.

"Get the money for Thomas," she told it. "Or find out how to."

This was a charm used to find out things, but she thought it might fetch money. And maybe it did work, because afterwards she got the idea of asking her father.

As she said, she would have to ask her father for money for them soon anyway. They lived frugally, postponing the day. Her money, the money they had lived on the twelve years of their marriage, was almost gone.

She washed her feet in raspberry soda and dusted her shoes with iron filings for luck. Then she drove to town. Her father was tall, deaf, and old to the age of fragility, with the scar of a World War I wound across his chest. He had once made a lot of money trading oil leases. He had once been married to a Houston socialite with whom he had a large family of sons and daughters, but in his forties had run away to the island with a much younger woman. Then they had married and produced another large family of sons and daughters, of whom Dinny was the youngest.

Every day he put on a Palm Beach suit and walked on the beach, where he picked up water-smooth rocks and slipped them into his pockets. He took them home and left them around on the polished mahogany tables with little trickles of sand going up to and coming away from them. He would wander from rock to rock, fingering them absently. His wife brushed the sand off and threw the rocks out.

To get him away from her mother, who would tell him not to, Dinny went walking with him on the beach. She had to shout in his ear to make him understand.

"To invest in a friend!" she shouted. His thin white hair blew forward in the wind.

But when he understood her, he wouldn't. "I have too many children," he said.

"But we don't need it," Dinny shouted into the wind. "None of us need it," though they themselves would soon.

And whether because her father knew this or for some other reason, all he would say was, "I have too many children."

Afterwards Dinny sat at home at the white enamel kitchen table and thought how if she had known, she could've told him it was for them. Outside the wind blew. The refrigerator cycled on in the white silence of the house. Soon it will be, she argued with nobody. Soon I will have to ask him for us. The refrigerator cycled off, and the drowsy house seemed to fall suddenly asleep. Except, she thought, he would find out.

And for a long time things were like this, a problem.

When the solution came—sideways—Dinny noticed how, and knew what she had been doing wrong. She had a dream. In the dream she realized from way down in her sleep that there was something dangerous out there, just beyond the fringe of oleander and crepe myrtle around the house. A bubble, like a soap bubble blown by all their sleeping breaths, rose trembling off the house. It would show they were there, she thought, so she reached up and touched it, to break it. Then she huddled back in her body, to see if whatever it was had seen them. It had. It was circling the house, coming up on them, coming to harm her and the children. She woke up.

It was very late. She was alone in the house with the children. Duff had gone to rehearsal and not come back, as often he didn't until morning. She knew she had been dreaming, and she knew she was awake—there was a patch of moonlight over her easel that she couldn't've dreamed—but in a terrifying way the dream continued. The thing was still out there. She could feel it. It had begun to coil itself around the house, looking for a way in. She got up, to do something, anything, to protect the children and herself.

She went after the thing through the dark house: she felt her way by following her fear. When she came into the kitchen she could feel it just on the other side of the back door. It was going to come in, too. She grabbed up what came to hand, which turned out to be felt-tip pens, and began to draw on the white enamel tabletop.

It came out a scaly dragon with a silly smile, in purple and green, like something out of a kids' color book. And as she drew she felt it gather itself up and pull away from the other side of the door. Leaving a smell of sulphur, it coiled back through the shrubbery the way it had come.

She went back to bed and back to sleep and slept solidly the rest of the night. When she woke up in the morning and remembered, she thought, I kept it out of the house.

Later, sitting at the table, she could see that the smile on the dragon was the smile on Duff, the way he had looked recently, and she knew that smile. All the little actresses, she thought.

She was angry and frightened, though she had no need to be. She had long ago fixed him so he could never leave her—not that she had ever believed he would. (His determination to have a family of his own was the second thing that had impressed Dinny about him when she met him at a Houston deb party. The first was that he was not wearing socks.)

Still, she had to turn him back to her, and make him pay. Before, she had simply gotten pregnant, but after Søren they had agreed that four were enough.

For several days she made peanut butter sandwiches and listened to children with the smallest part of her brain. The rest she held open and clear, like a ploughed field, remembering now, how to think. She barely saw Duff, who came in at dawn and slept all day, then left for rehearsal. She imagined that he knew she knew, that he was already nervous. He better be, she thought.

This came to her: a spell to cure madness, in which you split a live pigeon open and shove the bleeding heart against your madman's face, collect the blood in a cup as it runs down, and throw pigeon and cup into the river with a nickel for the spirits. It seemed like a good idea, though she did not think a nickel would be enough nowadays. In that way she fell to thinking about money again: the money she had, and the money she would need before long, and—because she had not thought about money for months without thinking about Thomas—the money she needed for Thomas.

And knew again to think of things not separately but pulling on each other as they always were. Then I can go to my father, she thought, and tell him it is for us.

Frightened, elated, she rode the days, listening to them and to herself. Then, one sunny morning, she woke up quite calm, got the children off to school, and while Duff was still asleep drove to town between the scattering dunes. At the bank she took out what they had left; then she drove on into the city on the freeway behind the loads of drilling pipe. Thomas was not at the shotgun house where he was staying, but she left the cashier's check in an envelope in the mailbox for him with a note scribbled on an old cash register receipt: "This is for real! An investment! From all of us. Busy this week. Come out next."

When she went on home, Duff had just gotten up and was wandering around the empty house naked as a Kewpie doll, wondering where she had gone. The man with the navy blue eyes, she thought, and how it was not really his fault.

They screamed at each other for hours, for days. He missed a rehearsal while they screamed at each other. They resolved to have quiet, rational discussions; he came home right after rehearsals, and they screamed at each other down the late nights.

"I had to," was the only explanation she gave. "I had to!" She seemed to be referring to some supernatural compulsion. In the end, Duff submitted to it. They were both exhausted.

Dinny agreed she would make no more financial decisions of such magnitude on her own. Duff broke off with the actress. They were united in terror about their bank balance. They made love again, intensely. Things changed; it was a new phase.

So that the Saturday Thomas drove out there in triumph, not having been since Dinny had left the money, he thought that she and the house were dressed for him. She had on a flow-ered skirt and bangle bracelets, had washed her tarnished-brass hair and let it hang loose, and the kitchen was astonishingly, gratifyingly clean. In the living room Duff interrupted the children's flute lesson to, he said in his formal way, assure Thomas of his own and his family's continuing support. How could it be otherwise, Thomas wondered in his happiness?

And for that matter, they are more like family to him now than ever. A successful manufacturer of small leather goods, Thomas drives out there in his own car without calling first now, goes leaping up the still-unpainted back steps to the kitchen, where Dinny may greet him a little abstracted now, from the white enamel table. Maybe she's dealing the tarot for some neighbor of theirs something just *has* to be done for, which makes Thomas glum, but what of it? Duff is laboriously the same; the children grow. It can only seem normal to Thomas.

As, too—hanging permanent in time—that triumphant day when he danced ecstatic to the music of love and fortune. The grown-ups sat down in the living room together—which they never had before—to listen to the children perform the flute song, "for Thomas," Duff said with a theatrical flourish. Dinny and Duff sat next to each other on the sofa, closer than Thomas had ever seen them; they held hands, fingers laced. They looked from the children to each other to Thomas and back, like people reunited after fire, flood, or other natural disaster. And the ragged breathy line of the children's melody wrapped around them all.

The Grand Duke
of Redonda

She says

We took the day sail to Redonda because, though Alex had never been there, he is the Grand Duke. Of course, the impulse had to be mine.

"Let's *go* there," I said—maybe just tired of hearing him talk about it. We were sitting in the bar of the hotel, where leaves of banana palms stuck in through jalousies under artificial green light.

"There's nothing there," Alex said, lifting a skinny shoulder. It was a heap of rocks in the Caribbean. "Absolutely nothing there." And yet, I could tell he was intrigued by the suggestion.

We had been on Antigua for a week and would be there for another week, and all he would do was sit talking in the hotel bar or lie closed in on himself in a shady deck chair with a shirt on and a towel over his legs. He turns red at the thought of the sun, so maybe he couldn't swim or snorkel with me. But neither would he walk on the beach with me when the sun went down (how banal), or sightsee (how vulgar), or go shopping (what did he want that they had?).

"Why do you come here?" I said finally, because he'd been coming there for years, though it was the first time he'd brought me.

"I like it," he said, with an expression that declared how little he liked anything. Alex likes his habits, I suppose, and them mostly because they are his habits.

But at that time I believed, as he did himself, that he might change, for my sake and his own. I gave him a bottle of sunscreen.

"What's that?" he said.

"Try a little," I said. "It might save you," but he wouldn't, even when he knew.

We spent a whole afternoon on that real island making up an alphabet of imaginary places: I remember Fat City, Xanadu.

71

Alex, being literary, was much better at this than I, which was probably why he wanted to do it. Poor Alex.

And maybe that immobility was mainly about drinking. Maybe he just wanted to lie there all day covered up, drinking rum drinks, though at the time that we went to Antigua, he was officially not drinking. I'd known him for years, and he had always drunk too much; then, shortly before we went to Antigua, his doctor had presented him with formal evidence: the beginning of clinical deterioration.

"I don't really care," Alex said. "But it is sort of a shock, after all these years, when it actually starts happening."

And for the sake of his liver or life alone, he would not have forgone so much as an ice cube.

But there was more. He had decided to marry me, as he'd announced earlier. God knows why. I wouldn't say he was in love with me, any more than I was with him, though we've always been fond of each other. I suppose, to put it nicely, I met his requirements: my wife, the (retired) ballerina (she teaches); I listened to him, which he needed; I tolerated him, which could be difficult. We'd been friends for so long. Of course, this does not sound like a marrying relationship to me now, but at the time, puzzling my way around him, around us, I thought, maybe. *He* seemed to see it so clearly, like one of his neatly polished stories. So I said I might, but not with the drinking. So he took me to Antigua and made this attempt.

Not drinking meant he had switched from whiskey to rum because he didn't like it as well, we had only one bottle of wine with dinner, and he didn't drink after dinner. Most nights he could walk back to the room by himself, climb the terraced hillside with me under the stars. In the mornings we woke early: the donkeys and the roosters.

"You know, it's amazing," he said one enameled blue A.M. as we descended the hill to breakfast. "There are mornings. I haven't had mornings for years."

Another time he snarled, "You're right, dammit, you're *all* right." He meant, besides me, his internist, his psychiatrist, and his mother. "It's good to feel good."

Alex does have a mother. His father, an engineering professor famous where engineering professors are famous, was so convinced that he himself was a yokel that he left the rearing of their only son to his Russian immigrant wife. She, poor woman, sent him to public school in the nineteen-fifties dressed in a suit, a starched white shirt, and a tie. She also taught him Russian—to speak Russian as a child in the nineteen-fifties in the heartland of the U.S.—and she taught him chess, which he played in tournaments in those days. I suppose his eventual insistence on everything that distinguishes him from other people was understandable.

When he was a freshman in college, he brooded publicly, wore black ascots, and wanted to be a poet; by the time he was an upperclassman he also aspired with faint disdain to be a professor of Russian literature; and he became both of those. Three books of poetry and an endowed chair later, he wanted to own certain rare books which he could do only by becoming an antiquarian book dealer, so he became that, too. But all of this becoming hasn't helped him much.

In a conversation we've had more than once, I ask him earnestly, "Are you happy with yourself?"

He says, "Christ, no." And when I tell him he might find out how to be happy in himself, he scowls at me to let me know I've said something silly and boring.

Dramatic, he goes on enacting the ideas of his youth.

And so he vacationed on an island, Antigua. Where in the evenings, he pretended not to drink, we ate, and he smoked the best cigars, one after another, in the dining room and the bar. He also told amusing stories to whoever would listen, stories in which he himself always played some part.

He says

A curious story, this island where Susan and I hope to land

tomorrow—if we can actually go ashore. Well, I will tell you if you want to hear.

It came about in this way. Perhaps a hundred years ago, an Englishman named Ewart landed on the island, a small island named unremarkably from old Spanish charts, Redonda. He claimed it as his own, which apparently, no country having seen reason to lay claim to it, he could do. Like the Brookses did Sarawak, you know Sarawak? No?

Well, the British Foreign Office likes to assume that Redonda belongs to them, but they don't like to talk about it because they aren't sure. So Ewart, this Englishman, could and did claim the island for himself and name himself its emperor. He called himself Emperor Gamaliel I, and shortly afterwards—to establish the succession, you see—he abdicated in favor of his infant son, whom he proclaimed Emperor Gamaliel II. It is through this man, the son, that I became connected with Redonda.

Besides the island, one gathers, the Ewarts did not own much by then. The old man, something of a yachtsman, genteel background but no more, knocked around the islands; the younger became a sort of literary man in London, where he gradually came upon hard times. At some point, as Emperor Gamaliel II, he began exercising his imperial power to create a complete peerage of Redonda—dukes, earls, the lot. In the beginning, perhaps, he invented these titles to amuse his more successful literary friends. The title that I bear, for instance, was first borne by a famous Welsh poet who was a sort of drinking friend of the Emperor in London. Eventually, though, Ewart seems to've passed them out to slight acquaintances, people he met casually in bars, anybody who'd buy him a drink. Nobody knows how many of these peerages there are, and probably most of the people he elevated to them thought they had no foundation in reality at all.

But on the splendid early occasion that Ewart created the famous poet the first Grand Duke Marlais of Redonda, Marlais being his middle name, the poet sat down at the bar and wrote two short poems for his Emperor, called "Epigrams of Fealty." They were subsequently published as a little book, which subsequently became very rare.

Some years ago, a copy of that little book came into my possession. By that time, both the famous poet and Emperor Gamaliel II were dead, and the "Epigrams of Fealty" were not universally believed to be authentic compositions of the great poet. Which affected the value of my find, you see.

Now at the time that the poems were written, there had also been present another friend of Emperor Gamaliel II, a man named Holdsworth, Ewart's closest friend, and at the time of which I speak, Holdsworth was still alive. He was, in fact, Ewart's heir. The two men had lived together for many years, and Ewart had made Holdsworth his literary executor and so forth, left him whatever little he had. So I looked him up in his London flat and went to see him.

It was a terrible hole—empty bottles and moldy plates— you couldn't sit on a chair—stuff stacked all around the floor. At that time I think Holdsworth was writing a memoir of Ewart; whether he ever finished it I don't recall hearing. And he had absolutely no money. I have no idea what he lived on.

"You want to see Ewart?" he said. I said I thought Ewart was dead.

" 'E is." Holdsworth plowed away a pile of stuff off the bookcase and showed me this bronze vase full of ashes and bits of bone.

" 'Ere 'e is. Ewart, Alex. 'E's come about the two little poems, the 'Epigrams of Fealty,' remember those? Alex, meet Ewart, 'is late Imperial Majesty of Redonda."

I said I thought they usually sealed those things up, I didn't think you were allowed to keep them in houses.

"Not," Holdsworth said. " 'E's waiting for mine. When I go. Going to be cremated same as 'im, and they're going to put mine in with 'is. Mix 'em up, mix 'em up."

Holdsworth is dead now, so presumably they're mixed up. Well, Holdsworth agreed, for five pounds and the notary's fee, to write out his account of how the epigrams came to be written, to have it notarized, and to deliver it to my hotel. This was a small place, owned by an Australian friend of mine—that's another story—and in case I wasn't in when Holdsworth came, I left the money with the Australian. I didn't dare give it to Holdsworth beforehand because I was afraid he'd get too drunk to write it.

I did leave him a bit more money than I'd promised, because he looked like he could use it, and when he got it, the Australian said, he was so appreciative he sat down there in the little hotel lobby and wrote out, on a piece of a brown paper bag, the patent of nobility making me the second Grand Duke Marlais.

And that's how I came to be the Grand Duke of Redonda, the island to which we sail tomorrow.

She says

(I fill in, twine around, frame.) We rented a boat; we embarked; we had what passes with us for a quarrel.

The boat was a smallish, new-looking yawl sailed by a black Martinique man named Nini, who told us that he had been all around the islands and to South America shrimping and to New Orleans for the Mardi Gras. Since I sail a little, I crewed, while Alex, who doesn't, sat with his feet up, all knobbly knees and elbows. We tacked out of the harbor and set sail; then I took the tiller and sat down with Alex, and we looked back at Antigua, which was gradually turning into a picture postcard behind us.

I made the kind of remark that, if I think about it before, I know he thinks is banal, except that I refuse to censor my remarks to Alex's taste. I said something about how exciting it is, when you're finally far enough out from land that you don't feel attached to it anymore, you're on your own on the sea.

Alex, who inclined to Briticisms even then, said, "It's a bloody relief. All that green growth crawling around. I always feel slightly nauseated by it."

Since there are limits to what I will let him get away with, I said, "I love the flowers. Magenta, flame."

He laughed. "The bougainvillea? Those crude colors?"

Supercilious bastard. I had one of those regular moments when I wondered, how *could* I live with a man like that. I didn't say anything, though. If I'd told him he was a supercilious bastard, as I have on other occasions, he would simply have agreed, preening a little. He means to be. And such admissions are disarming, hold out hope in their peculiar way. I suppose I revenge myself now with program notes, my interpretation, the last untriumphant word.

Nini came aft to take the tiller from me and settled down, smiling. Afterwhile I realized that he smiled continuously, that it had nothing to do with his real state of mind. He asked why we wanted to go to Redonda. This made Alex happy, put him on his own ground with the man.

"It's a long story," Alex said, as if he might not tell it.

"Good," the man said. "Good. I like stories." Alex took out cigars and offered the man one.

Nini took it and looked at it. "Thank you," he said. "It is very good. I will have it later, if you don't mind. The boat." He put the cigar in his pocket.

Alex nodded and cut his, gratified, the teller of stories, bestower of fine cigars. "What is it?" he said, "just a pile of rocks? Have you seen it?"

"Yes, that's it, a pile of rocks. I have seen it, but not near. There might be guano there. Otherwise, nothing. Poison fish are in the waters around."

"Poison fish," Alex said.

"They say that," the man said. "I have not seen them. Fish that you cannot eat."

That pleased Alex. He savored it for a moment, hand on the

gunwale holding the cigar, poised elegantly like some seabird ready to take off. Then he presented again that entombed experience, the story of how he became the Grand Duke of Redonda. After the trip, he had another episode, what happened to him there.

He says

I knew from a distance. I knew before I knew what. The whole experience was one of those classic successions of events that you see coming, that gather and rise to some climax after which everything is different? Boring sort of shape, really, but there it was. As we drew near to Redonda, we were passing among other islands. The larger ones were densely overgrown, perhaps watered by springs, the smaller ones nearly barren, with only a few scrubby bushes clinging to cracks in the rock, and what I saw excited me, though I could not have said why. At each of several such small islands, I asked our boatman, "Is it smaller than that?"

I know he was amused. "Oh, yes," he would say at each one, "very much smaller," and I felt an emotion that—perhaps you will not believe me when I say—I hardly recognized. After a while I suspected it was hope.

Coming around a large island, we sighted Redonda at a distance, lying low, barely visible amid the waves. I could hardly contain my excitement. It seemed at every moment as if we were just about to come upon it, but the island proved farther away than I thought. When, however, we were able to get a closer look at it, it appeared as a smallish heap of cinders that grew only a little larger as we approached. From the sea view, there seemed to be nothing at all on it. The hope I had hardly begun to identify held.

The island was simply a pile of loose, ash-colored rocks, maybe fifty yards across, roughly conical, with a bite out of one side. I watched, fearing to see, not knowing what I feared.

The boatman said he couldn't go in farther, he could drop the anchor there and we could swim in if we wanted to. Except for the sound of the waves there, it was absolutely quiet. There was no surf to speak of—there was no beach. At what must've been a distance of about a hundred and fifty feet, Redonda rose up before me, blazing hot, apparently barren, inhospitable, and mine.

Now, I tell you this so that you will understand how entranced I was. I am not a good swimmer. I am not remotely athletic. I don't do these sorts of things, but I removed the contents of my pockets, took off my shoes and socks, tied my shoes together, and climbed over the side of the boat into the water, without listening to any of the advice that was offered to me or thinking about how deep the water might be or what the bottom might be like or anything else. In fact, the water was not deep, and after a few splashes I walked slowly to shore, leaving Susan and the boatman talking about lunch, of all things. I'm afraid I was rather rude—my dear? I remember shouting something like, "You are not going to eat on my island!"

And then I set foot on Redonda. What can I say to express the peace that I felt, beginning the minute I stepped out of the water onto that dry, dry land? I knew only that I had never felt remotely as serene, as I never have since. At the waterline were the usual decayed bits of palm and other flotsam, but above the waterline I looked up onto a landscape of absolute lunar aridity. I put on my shoes and started to climb, with water running down off me into them, so that I soon squished with every step.

The rocks shifted and slid under my weight, but what I discovered myself looking for would've been between the rocks, and so I looked there as I climbed, and the farther I went up, the more exultant I felt. To me, unathletic as I am, it seemed rather heavy going and a long climb to the summit, but I went on as if in a dream, and when I made it and looked down on all sides of the island, I knew, because I saw, what I'd been hoping for.

The place was utterly uninhabited. There was not a green

plant on the island, not a lizard, not an insect among the rocks. Nothing. Baked motionless under the sun, the island baked back the air above it into hot shimmers.

How can I describe my feeling? Like God after the end of the world? I presided over the place of burnt bones, perfectly solitary. I thought of Ewart's father and laughed. Nobody, perhaps not even Ewart, had fully appreciated the humor of the man's claim. What I experienced was the discovery of a virtual certainty. That island has lain there unchanged for how long, a geologic age? It's not forever, but it's long enough for me. The sky does things over it, the waves do things around it, there are storms, lightning, wind, calms. And they are all nonsense on this island, because it's ruined already, impervious to ruin. It can only be covered over when the polar ice caps melt, or be thrust apart in some unlikely geologic upheaval.

I knew then that I had anticipated and recognized the island before I knew why, as the native territory of my soul. You see, at this time in my life various people—doctors, Susan here, with the best of intentions—were trying to tell me that what I knew, what I *knew* was real in me was only a sickness I ought to get over. And then, there it was, objective in the world, unarguable as a pile of rocks.

I felt more normal than I had for a long time, perhaps ever. I went down the summit a little way on the other side and sat down on the burning rocks, confident in what I was for maybe the first time in my life: king of the mountain of clinkers by the railroad tracks to hell. I don't know how long I sat there. It seemed like a long time, even more like the beginning of a long time. I only came back because I wanted a drink.

Cheers.

She says

I didn't hear that story until a couple of years later in a London wine bar—his old friend, sitting with others around a low round table. Of course, meanwhile I had my own version of what happened on Redonda, if a vaguer and more tentative one.

I could see that he was affected by the place, some desperate quality of it. Still, I ate my lunch on board before I stripped to bathing suit and thongs to splash ashore, where I chose my path more comfortably along the waterline. Alex describes the place without exaggeration: there was nothing there but rocks. Shading my eyes with my hand, scanning the face of the heap, I walked around to the other side of the island. I saw him sitting up there, in the posture of a blue funk. He was not happy to see me.

He called down, "I'm staying."

In a general way, I got the idea—not that we would have to drag him kicking and screaming back to the boat. Some hardened refusal of the rest of the world.

"Okay," I yelled and walked on along the shore, back towards the boat, knowing also that *we* were through, in the way we had tried to be. I have to admit that, thinking only of myself, I was relieved.

On the boat, Nini looked at me curiously out of little smiling eyes and talked about the countries he had visited. People in the U. S., he said, expect too much. Afterwhile, Alex came over the crown of the hill and down towards us, with his clothes dried into strange shapes from the way he'd been sitting.

"Thirsty," he said, when he stood streaming on board. He began to drink the rest of the beer.

He didn't say anything about what had happened until we were back on Antigua, in the taxi climbing the steep cobbled hill to the hotel. Then he said, "I've decided to move to London. To drink."

He did, and lives there now. I see him when I go over. He claims to be dying, which is sad if true, but suits him. He looks just the same to me.

Give

He's a finder, the Pope. We call him the Pope cause his name is John Paul, and cause he's a biker—biker's got to have a nickname. Course the Pope don't have a bike right now. What the Pope's got is a wife and nine kids and a job driving a gravel truck. Still, scooter trash. And the Pope is a finder. He's always looking around him, so he sees, really sees, what's there.

One time he's driving down the road with his old lady in this '81 Ford of his and he thinks he's got tire trouble, so he pulls over, gets out. Fat guy, slings his belly out over his jeans, and he's got one of them Fu Manchu mustaches, hanging down. And he's walking around the car looking, like he always does, and he sees something shiny laying in the dirt, bends down, picks it up, and it's a three-quarter carat diamond. Just loose, like that, where it fell out of somebody's ring. Where you and me would've seen a level place to crank a jack, set one of them motorcycle boots right on top of the sombitch, the Pope sees it, and it's a diamond.

He knew, right away, what it was. His old lady was sitting up there in the front seat like she's gonna make him jack her up with the car. She's something else, wears them big dresses you could crawl under there with her. I wouldn't mind. She's got a mouth on her, too.

The Pope shows her this diamond and she says, "That's a piece of glass, John Paul. Rhinestone. Or one of them cubic zirconias you get at the discount house, thirty-nine ninety-five."

But the Pope don't say nothing, just reaches out with that diamond and scratches a big x right across the windshield on her side of the car. Cause he knew.

He sold that diamond, too. Probably bought meat for the freezer. The Pope is always cooking meat. They live in one of them quadriplexes with the master bedroom down the end of the hall, and his old lady is always laying down back in the bedroom, having a baby. So the Pope does the cooking and he's always cooking meat. You ought to see their place—rug rats and yard-highs everywhere, and the Pope trying to keep them in line. Can't do it, though. But when he serves out what he's cooked himself—he gets off to this—the piece of meat he gives you is just how he's feeling about you that day.

What the Pope can find ain't only gold and jewels—it's all kind of valuable things. You'll be driving along the interstate with him, not seeing nothing but shopping centers and housing developments, and the Pope'll look over at a sudden little valley with a few trees at the bottom and say, "Creek down there, got fish in it." I never tried him on any of those, but Ernie—that's another friend of ours—he says the Pope can really pick the spots.

Course most people don't pay the Pope no mind, cause he don't seem real smart. Sometimes he can't hardly talk: he sorta jitters. Or he can't understand you real good cause he can't remember what words mean. Might be something wrong with him in the head—one of them road accidents or getting beat up too much did something to his brain. But maybe he never learned. Ernie says the Pope's just a hillbilly.

Whatever he is, people disbelieve the Pope to their loss. One time we went to—he's into these pioneer swap meets. Like a flea market, only people trading flintlock rifles and them enormous-mother Bowie knives. All kinds of stuff there, wagon wheels and anvils, axes and churns. A whole log cabin, reassembled on the spot. And this one old man had a bunch of arrowheads and clay jars and other Indian things spread out on an Indian blanket on the ground, and the Pope is real interested in Indian stuff. Soon as he looked at it, he seen this pipe, long clay pipe with a decorated stem, laying there on the blanket, and he got real excited, like he does.

"That's old!" he says. "That's real old!"

Old man, skin so thin the blood of his face is showing through. Smiles, kinda humoring the Pope.

And the Pope handles this pipe, holds it up and looks at it

real close—he wears these little round John Lennon glasses—
looks at this pipe through those glasses like he never seen
anything like it before. When he's through, he puts it back in
place on the blanket like it was a new baby.

Then he asks the guy if he means to swap it. Course this
gives the old guy another curl—cause it's a swap meet, see.

So the old guy asks him what he's got, and the Pope holds
up his finger, "Wait. Don't go away. Just wait," and we go back
to the car for this pair of Indian tomahawks the Pope had, that
he always thought a lot of. And all the way there and back the
Pope gabbles on about how old that pipe is.

"Man," he says, "that's the oldest thing I ever seen."

"How old, you figure?" I ask him. "Older than America?
Older than Jesus Christ? Older than the Bible?"

But of course the Pope don't know about any of that. He just
knows that pipe is the oldest thing he ever seen.

That old red-faced man, he liked them two tomahawks. He
traded that pipe to the Pope for them two tomahawks like he
believed he got the best of that deal. Afterwards he said he got
that pipe about eight, ten years ago from a man in Louisiana
told him he robbed it one night with a bunch of other stuff
out of an Indian mound.

And the Pope was just as pleased. I'm telling you, he handled
that pipe with respect. And—this is the kicker—later him and
Ernie took it to a professor Ernie found out could tell how old
a thing was, and this professor kept it for a while and did
something to it that didn't hurt it none, and you know what he
told the Pope? Told him that pipe was five thousand years old.
Wanted him to donate it to the natural history museum. Had
to explain to the Pope that means *give*. Pope says uh-uh. Man
like me can't afford to donate nothing except to his wife and
children. He's still got that pipe, wrapped up in paper towels
on the top shelf of his closet.

So if there was a vein of gold in this county, which they
knew there was, the Pope would be the man to find it. They

been looking for it for years. All them big geologists and min-
ing engineers—I read about it in the paper. They knew where
it went out of sight over in the next county, figured it cropped
up somewhere over here. I guess I told the Pope, or he already
knew. Guys on the job were talking about it.

Then one day the Pope drove his truck up on the construction site where they were building that extension to the highway, and he seen it, just seen that vein of gold, striping across
a fresh bulldozer cut. He got real excited, like he does—I
wasn't there, but he showed it to me later—and he got down
and went over and tried to tell the site engineer and the
surveyors.

"That's that," he says. "See? That's gold! That's that vein
of gold!"

But they wouldn't pay him no mind. Just laughed at him, the
way guys like that are gonna do at a guy like the Pope. "That's
pyrites," they told him. "Fool's gold, son." And I reckon they
had another laugh talking about it over lunch—one of them
crazy truckers. Fat guy with the evil-looking mustache.

But the Pope knew it was gold. He went back with a pick
and shovel the next day—being a state job they weren't working on Saturday—and he shovels him up a bucket of that gold
dirt. He showed me where it was, and we went out there at
night and loaded up half my pickup full, brought it home. I
thought, way he's talking about it, least I might get me a nug-
get, have it made into an earring. But there wasn't no nuggets,
just rocks and dirt with gold dust sprinkled through them. It
was gold, all right, though. The Pope took some of it to a place
to have it what they called assayed, and sure enough, he got a
letter to prove it. They told him it was good as that ore they
mine in South Africa. Course it takes tons, and you have to do
a bunch to it before you actually get any gold. They leaned on
him pretty hard to tell them where it came from. He thought
they had a suspicion it was from around here, but he wouldn't

tell them. Told them he brought it back from Colorado a while ago.

After that he pretty much lost interest in it—soon's he found out he wasn't gonna buy his old lady an El Camino with it. So far as he's concerned, it's just a pile of shiny dirt laying out back of his carport.

But some day when the boss or some engineering guy's been on one of our asses, the Pope and me'll be driving home together and come up towards the spot on the new highway where that vein of gold is—you can't see it anymore. The state done covered it over with about a million yards of concrete. But the Pope'll sorta look at me up from under those little glasses. And he'll be paying attention, hunched over with his head cocked around, waiting, and then he'll say, "That's it! There it's at!" and all *right*. He can feel it, he says, like a little thump. Like driving over one of them expansion joints on the highway.

The Catfish-Head Tree

They had always understood that their mother had been un-
faithful to their father, though they couldn't actually remember
anything about it. Lee, who was the oldest, who had been six
when their father threw her out, was the only one who even
remembered her. He said she wore a red-printed apron, the
kind that looks like a shirt on backwards, with red—later he
learned it was called piping—around the armholes. One time
he told Hardin, who was the middle one, that she smelled like
corn bread baking, "with a lot of sugar in it," which was the
way he liked it.

"You can't tell that," Hardin said. They were maybe fourteen
and twelve, out after school in the wintertime, digging post-
holes by hand on the small cattle ranch their father had won
the down payment for in a VA hospital poker game before they
were born.

But Lee, who would never back off from anything, said he
could tell. And Lee always got to be the authority when they
talked about her because Hardin himself couldn't remember
her, though he thought he ought to've been able to—he had
been four.

They kept trying to figure it out, just between the two of
them, what had happened. Danny, who was the youngest, was
not interested in her, or they did not include him: he had only
been two, and he was not as close to them as they were to
each other.

Howcome, Hardin said another time, in the barn, where
they were resting from shoving down the big rectangular bales
of hay, "you s'pose it's such a big secret?" It was true, nobody
ever said anything about it that they heard, though everybody
out there in the country and in town where they went to
school must've known, something. The woman who had been
their mother lived in a neighboring town and was remarried,
to a dentist, as their father was also remarried, to Dixie.

Lee laughed his cynical laugh. "Fraid of him," he said, as if

Hardin ought to've known that. Their father, who beat up on them regularly, was always in some quarrel with one of his neighbors.

Whatever their mother had done, Hardin and Lee decided, their father had probably driven her to it. And the thought that she had just gone ahead and done it pleased Hardin. He was named for her—Hardin had been her maiden name—and he believed he must be like her, hard-headed and hard-assed.

They only saw her the one time, one summer day when they were in their teens, after they'd gone broke on cattle during the drought and moved to town. They had just moved into the long low cream brick house, called ranch style, that they got from selling the real ranch, and she called up and said she'd like to come by. Their father was selling real estate by then and wasn't home—maybe she'd counted on that. And Dixie, who was their stepmother, hospitable, sympathetic Dixie, said, why, yes, do come.

Her name was Helene, Mrs. Kupferman. She was tall and blonde, like they were, but except for that they did not resemble her—in the face they all looked like their father, who was said to be handsome. She was dressed up for the visit, in a black dress, and she sat in the living room on the new modern swimming-pool colored chair drinking iced tea from a yellow plastic glass with a sprig of mint sticking out of it. The three of them, Hardin already the biggest, sat crowded in a row on the sofa, shuffling for some place under the new Danish modern coffee table to put their Levi-ed shins, their boots and canvas high-tops, trying to believe that this was their mother. Lee was the one who always wore boots.

And Lee claimed, years later, to've liked her, but Hardin had felt nothing for her, which confused him at the time. Because he had expected to feel kin to her, but when she was there, a quiet-spoken, kind of high-toned woman who chatted with Dixie and looked at them, he couldn't feel any connection with her at all. She didn't stay long, and afterwards she seemed less real to him than the woman he had always believed in, who had given his father what he deserved.

His father had a fit when he found out she'd been there, but that sort of thing never fazed Dixie. "They have a right to know her," she said, forcing the words out on little huffs of breath, flying her dignity like a flag.

Dixie was the only luck they'd ever had, parentwise. "He could've married *anybody*," Hardin said once after they were grown, "the way he was." It had been right after the bust-up with Helene, and Lee claimed Dixie had only married their father to get them, since she had been crippled in a farm accident in her youth and could not carry children of her own, an explanation Hardin did not believe. But however the connection had come about, Dixie had coddled them insofar as she thought good for them, chivvied them into whatever manners or morals or education any of them had, and stood up to their father when she dared. How she put up with the old man they could scarcely understand.

"Oh," she would say, rolling her china-doll eyes and flinging up her fat hands, as if at something halfway funny.

If it hadn't been for Dixie, none of them would've kept in touch at all out there, once they got away, though Danny was the only one who did it right: Mother's Days and her birthdays, Thanksgivings and Christmases. Danny was a computer programmer, and Hardin and Lee had a joke about how Danny was the only one of them that turned out any good.

"Got him a new Japanese pick-em-up truck with them big tires and a condo full of electronic shit," Hardin told Lee over the phone. Hardin, who drove a truck for a living, was staying in a trailer at the time and could've gotten everything he owned into a footlocker, Lee probably less.

Lee played poker for a living and had been married four times, and once they didn't hear from him for a whole wife.

But Hardin would sometimes, on an odd day off—a week-day too wet to work or something—drive the six hours out there just to see Dixie, sit around and drink coffee and smoke cigarets with her for a while, maybe take off before the old man came home.

And one time, Hardin asked Dixie what really happened be-tween their father and their real mother. Sitting at the formica breakfast bar, he leaned the Mediterranean-style chair back on two legs and said, "You know. When they split up." He had been divorced twice himself and believed he could see these people as just another couple, not particularly his mother and father at all.

But Dixie only shook her head a little so that her cheeks wobbled and did something with her mouth that meant she didn't approve—of whatever had happened, or simply of his asking her that. Hardin didn't know which. She got up and went into the kitchen, poured more coffee, and that was that.

"Maybe she didn't know," Lee said to Hardin. "How would she, except what he told her?"

Then one night down in the city—it was almost midnight—Hardin had been out for a few beers after work and gone and eaten some barbecue, and he walked in to the phone ringing, and it was Dixie.

She'd been trying to reach him all evening, she said, but she didn't sound more than just ordinarily fussed. She might've been making some commonplace request—come out here and move that sofa for me, come out here and trim trees. She said, "Come out here and help me! *Your* father is trying to kill me."

Standing half-drunk and tired in the empty little efficiency he had only recently moved into, with the wrecked motorcycle he had no place else for filling the living room, Hardin could scarcely take it in. No violent thing his father tried to do

would've surprised him, but he had never spared a doubt that
Dixie could handle the old man.

She was all right, Hardin got that. But her stream of talk was
not telling him what he wanted to know, and he could not
form the questions to ask her.

In the end, he thought he'd best just get on the road and
said, "I'll be there," and hung up. It would take him the rest of
the night to drive out there.

He did call the boss up at home, woke him, it seemed
like, which gave Hardin a certain pleasure, and told him he
wouldn't be in. Then he took a leak and, limping a little on the
bad knee, went back out into the humid August night.

The interior of the ten-year-old LTD was full of empty beer
and soda cans and fast-food trash. Sitting down low there after
being up high in the cab of the gravel truck all day still felt
familiarly strange, and at first Hardin just drove, concentrating
on not doing anything he might get stopped for.

But when he hit the freeway, with the windows down because the AC needed a little work, his head began to clear. He
tried to tune the radio to some rock and roll, but there was
something wrong with it. He wished for about the millionth
time that he had a good stereo in the car, like they had in the
truck he drove, and thought how he could buy himself one
any payday he remembered to, but what a waste it'd be to put
it into that old car.

An eighteen-wheeler passed him in the thump and rush of
displaced air. Hardin flicked his lights to let the guy know he'd
cleared him and thought of what his father said to him every
time he saw him lately, if he said anything: "Are you still driving a truck?" As if selling real estate or having failed as a cattle
rancher was so much better. Long ago, their father had been a
war hero, blowing up most of a company of Japanese on a box-
shaped island in the Pacific before being wounded and sent
home. Hardin cast his mind back to when he'd fallen in love

with driving, for what it could do for him when they'd lived out in the country. He thought how it was: you started doing something because you liked it; then one day you realized it'd turned into a job.

He smoked cigarets one after another in the alternating spaces of darkness and light from the lights on the freeway.

Afterwhile, he stopped for gas and coffee at a Stop-n-Go. Paying the brown-skinned clerk, he felt for the guy: commonest job to get shot doing. Back in the car he stuck the warm styrofoam cup between his thighs.

As he got closer to whatever he was going to, he fell to thinking about how his father was and how much it had cost them all in life. He remembered the time his father had accused Lee of selling hay out of the barn, when Lee probably would've done it if he'd known how, but he hadn't, and his father had whipped Lee with a belt until the backs of his legs were covered with red welts. He thought of Lee laying up in bed on his stomach in the smell of Cloverleaf salve saying in a dead voice, "It doesn't matter what I do." He thought of how Lee had looked the last time he'd seen him, when Lee had called up from the bus station, just in from Reno, in shirtsleeves with no luggage, broke and shrugging, having just walked away from whatever he'd had there. That was Lee.

But afterwards, smoking another cigaret with the ash flying out and back in on the wind, Hardin remembered—he and Lee are waiting to die from this—spraying cattle with DDT for screwworms when they were just kids, their father too, with their shirts off, getting soaking wet from the spray and letting it dry on them over and over, like sweat. Give his father credit, he didn't know any better—nobody in those days knew. As Lee said, their only hope was that DDT was stored in fat, and there wasn't an ounce of fat on any of them then. Hardin could see them as they had been, three skinny little boys and a lean mean man, trying to turn that piece of raw pasture into a ranch. They'd done it, too, for all the good it was. In the end there were houses built on that land.

Hardin held the steering wheel loosely with big scarred hands and thought how he'd hated his father in those days and for years, and didn't really anymore. Punched it out on other people, he supposed. Now he tried to stay out of trouble—he even gave up eating red meat for a while, awhile back, in an effort to become more peaceful. Now when he thought of his father, it was mostly just with this feeling of waste and regret.

Hardin rested his elbow out the window, his arm bare to the shoulder, and the air flowed in the armhole, ballooning the shirt on him. Just that morning he had ripped out the sleeves with his knife.

He thought about the last time his father had ever hit him. Lee had already dropped out of college and left home, and one Sunday afternoon in cold weather, Hardin had been sitting in the living room with Dixie, and he had gotten up restlessly and said, just kind of thinking out loud to her, about how he didn't know if he really wanted to major in business, he liked some of the other courses better.

His father had been going out the sliding glass doors that opened onto the patio, but he had stopped and turned around. He had stood there, a little bent-kneed, arms down at his sides and out, like a man who's had to carry two loaded buckets for so long he doesn't know when he doesn't anymore—though he'd been in the real estate business a good five years by then. He had on khaki work clothes, too, like he used to wear on the ranch and still wore when he worked outside around the house.

"Heaw!" he hollered, like you hollered at a calf or a dog, and Dixie jumped, scattering crochet hooks and little flat bobbins of thread. "As long as I pay the bills," he shouted, "you'll study what I tell you to study!" His face was crimped with anger.

And this really burned Hardin, not that it was any different from the way his father had always talked to them, but because up until the time they had sold the ranch they had all worked, getting up at 4 A.M. in the winter dark to do chores before school, coming right home after school, though he and Lee had wanted to play football so bad, and weekends and summers. And Hardin knew damn well—his father often said so himself—that the sale of the ranch had given them everything they had, including his father's business. So Hardin said in his most reasonable way, "Now, wait a minute."

"Shut your trap," his father ordered him, and then Hardin felt stupid, as if he had actually believed that all by himself he could change the way his father talked to him.

But this only made Hardin want to show his father what a wrong way to talk really was, so he said to him, very deliberately, "Screw you."

And his father, who was several inches shorter than Hardin but pounds heavier in those days, punched him hard in the stomach. It knocked the wind out of him, doubled him over in that paralyzed panic that stops your time, while Dixie, in her own, fluttered somewhere out of reach, saying, "Maynard! What have you done!"

Then Hardin drew the breath that revs it all up again, and there he was in the living room on Sunday afternoon with Dixie and his father, straightening up, wiping his eyes on his plaid flannel shirtsleeve, with his father standing nervously away from him.

Hardin took a step towards his father, who tucked his chin into his shoulder a little. "Now, Hardin!" Dixie cried.

And Hardin had said to his father, "If you *ever* lay a hand on me again."

His father had snorted and gone out the sliding glass door, pushing it to, hard, behind him, but he never had hit Hardin again. In fact, it seemed to Hardin like his father had barely spoken to him since, though that could not be true in nearly twenty years. Hardin never had changed his major. He dropped out of school later on that year.

And this memory, like the others, made Hardin sad, because, though you could not blame anybody else for the things you yourself had done, he thought he could see how one thing had led to another, and there did not seem to've been any way to stop it.

From the off ramp he looked down onto a roof that had The B-Back painted on it in big white letters. It was the first beer store on the edge of a wet county, where the brothers had always stopped off and bought a six-pack apiece when they were headed home. Lee's joke was that as long as they always did it, Dixie wouldn't know they were drunked up, she'd just think that was the way they were. The place was closed, not that Hardin would've wanted to drink this time anyway.

Down on the blacktop it was dark and there was nobody. Feeling out the familiar hills and curves with his body, Hardin missed his motorcycle. He'd wrecked it, also his knee, sliding into a road grader, but they'd put the knee back together, sort of. It pained him after the long day in the truck and the night's driving, and he tried to stretch the leg out a bit, but there wasn't room. He'd been off work four months with it. They said he was lucky to have the leg.

He could pick out the landmarks on this road without having to see them. He passed the abandoned gas station built out of petrified wood, sitting by itself at the top of a long hill, and thought about Edna, his second wife, and his children, the blond boy and girl, the way they had looked the last time he had seen them. He tried to remember exactly why they had broken up, but he couldn't. Right then, it seemed like something that had just happened. He passed the turnout where he had found the deer's skeleton, years ago. He ran through towns their high school played in football, where there was no light on but the blinking yellow of the crossroads. He ran over rumbling bridges, crossing the same river over and over.

He ran into another sleeping white town cut longways by the road. It was the catfish-head tree town. He slowed to see the tree. There it was, a big old live oak at the edge of a weed-grown front yard—he could make out in the dark—still hung with catfish heads. Man fished for cat and hung the heads in the tree from little lengths of line, till the whole tree was full of them. The year and a half that Hardin and Lee had both been in college and driven this part of the road home together, they would stop and look at those heads and try to guess how big different fish had been. Lee would swear that this or that one was a hundred pounds, two hundred pounds, and once Lee bet Hardin he wouldn't go knock on the back door—the front door being boarded up—and ask, so Hardin did. But the man who came to the door, a fat man with brown snaggle teeth, was real hot at being bothered about it, and said the reason he hung them heads up there was so damnfools wouldn't ask him how big that fish was. As if everybody else could figure it out, Hardin thought, and it was only you.

By the time he cruised into their town, the dark was beginning to thin out, and a few lights were on, of people who got up early. If he'd been home, he'd've been getting up himself. He drove past new houses and convenience stores, then past old houses and new banks. He rubbed his long jaw; he hadn't shaved for a couple of days, and he could barely tell where his sideburns ended. He drove past more new houses and convenience stores, and on out the other side. He could see as he came up on the cream brick house that all the lights were on. He turned into the long clay driveway. Along both sides of it, in full bloom, were the watermelon crepe myrtles they had brought from the ranch.

"I didn't dare go to bed!" Dixie said, locking the door from the carport behind him. A short, round-bottomed woman in stretch slacks and a flowered smock, she waddled into the kitchen ahead of Hardin, her rolling walk from a hip injury of long ago. Her hair, which used to be reddish, was white, but she had it rinsed a sort of pink at the beauty parlor.

"He came home at suppertime and started in on me!" she said cheerfully, as if reporting something pleasant or amusing. She wouldn't say what about. "Oh, it was nothing," she said. "Just something he thought." While she talked she moved around the kitchen, starting a fresh pot of coffee in the automatic coffee maker, getting things out of the refrigerator to make Hardin a sandwich without asking him if he wanted one.

From the kitchen he could see over the breakfast bar into the living room: a hardback book weighted open on the sofa by a large ashtray full of cigaret butts. When they had been older but still lived on the ranch, Dixie had taught school for a while, until she got fired for throwing a dance for Lee's class in their barn ("I did not get fired," she says. "They reinstated me, and then I quit").

The sandwich was going to be her homemade pimento cheese on white bread, the only kind of pimento cheese Hardin liked. "And he had been drinking," she confided.

That was how it went, the drinking and brooding, after which some offense would be taken. Sometimes you could see it coming for hours before you know what it would be about. When they were kids and he was like that, somebody would always get a licking. Hardin leaned against the kitchen counter and looked around at the new microwave, the all-electric stovetop, the oven in the wall. Though he had not been there for months, everything was familiar, down to the cup towels Dixie crocheted orange borders onto and the wrought-iron framed tiles to set hot things on, painted with orange mushrooms.

"And then when I didn't—oh, you know how your father is," she said, lowering her chin and shaking her head a little. "He went into the bedroom and got that pistol out of the nightstand!" Hardin knew that pistol, the Nambu automatic his father had brought home from the Pacific. He and Lee and Danny had been allowed to shoot targets with it.

"He keeps it there now," Dixie said. "He thinks somebody's going to rob the house while we're asleep, or murder us in our beds."

She cut the sandwich from corner to corner with the big French chef's knife Hardin had given her one year for a late Christmas present. Then she put the sandwich on one of the small yellow dishwasher-safe plastic plates and set it over by him on the counter.

"And then he commenced to wave that thing around at me while I was trying fix supper!" she said. "I was afraid it'd go off by accident, and there's no telling what might've happened if hadn't Billy Joel come driving up the driveway, and Maynard went out to talk to him and took that pistol with him. While he was out there I went around the house and locked the doors and went into the inside bathroom and stayed there."

So his father had the pistol. Hardin bit off one long corner of the sandwich.

"Oh, he did make a fuss," Dixie said. She lit one of the extra-long, extra-skinny menthol cigarets she smokes. They waited for the coffee to drip through.

He wouldn't've shot his way in, Hardin thought, or busted the patio doors, because he wouldn't've wanted to break up his own property.

"Afterwhile he went on off," Dixie said. "I think he's checked in over at the motel. He called from there, carrying on something ridiculous about how I'd locked him out of his own house. He's feeling sorry for himself now." She dragged fiercely on the little cigaret, inhaling about half of it at once. "If you can just get that gun away from him."

Hardin didn't think his father would want to shoot anybody anymore, either. He bit into the other half of the sandwich.

Dixie poured coffee into a mug that said on one side "I'm no good at all" and on the other "'till I've had my coffee" and sugared it just the way he liked it. She set the cup over next to him.

"What was it this time?" he said.

She took out another of the little cigarets and lit it off the butt of the old one. "Oh, it was the bingo!" she said. "You know I play bingo at the VFW on Tuesday night with Wail and Marie Sedky—Maynard won't go—and Wail always picks me up by himself because it's on the way from—that's the night he closes the store late—and then we go by and Marie's all ready, and we go on out there. And your father decided— he *accused* me of carrying on with Wail Sedky! He said we weren't playing bingo at all on Tuesday nights. Can you imagine that? When probably fifty people've seen me there every Tuesday night for four years except the time it snowed last winter, and then I was right here, as Maynard well knows. I told him that, but it just made him madder. Wail Sedky indeed!"

Headed back towards the string of green stucco cabins they called the motel, Hardin was thinking how his father wouldn't play bingo with Dixie or go out with her at all, wouldn't do hardly anything except sell a little real estate and watch TV, which he did with contempt and no consideration, switching programs off in the middle if he wanted to, whether anybody else was watching them or not. The streets of town were still mostly empty, though it was full light. An old man wearing baggy undershorts stood outside in front of a house watering a patch of dry brown grass with a green hose. Hardin thought how Dixie went her own way and had her own friends: people liked her, as they never much had Maynard. If there was anything she felt she'd missed out on in life, you'd never know it. Carrying on with another man, Hardin thought, what a ridiculous accusation to make against a woman like Dixie.

Then he remembered that his father had said the same thing about their real mother, and the shapes of things he had believed he knew wavered and dissolved. He recalled the blond woman sitting in the aqua chair all those years ago who did not seem like she had done what his father said. Maybe she hadn't, Hardin thought.

There came to him the rags of a memory he had not known he had, of his father shouting, "You done it! I know you done!" and his father shoving somebody Hardin couldn't see but knew was his mother against something that broke. That was the glass-fronted bookcase that afterwards, glass removed, had held dusty copies of *Farm and Ranch* and *Range Management,* and that even now was somewhere in the house: Dixie had painted it white and set green plants in it.

Feeling his memory opened up, Hardin tried, as he and Lee always had, to recall any man who might've come to the house or that she might've gone to see, though they had only had the one old broken-down pickup for years and years, and his father mostly drove that. What would she have done with the three of them while she had an affair, he wondered. When he thought about it in practical terms, he didn't see how she could've. He supposed he could go ask her and wondered how she would react to that. If she hadn't, he thought, as he turned into the motel parking lot, then she hadn't been the kind of person he thought she was at all.

Things shone in the glossy light like they did when he had taken acid or drank tequila. The place was called The Pines, on account of two scrubby evergreens of the kind they called cedar that grew one on each side of the entrance to the parking lot, but which he had learned were in fact not cedars at all but something else—he couldn't remember what. A red pickup truck and two cars sat in the parking lot, one of them his father's new cream-colored Oldsmobile. The cabins were the pale green of cheap nylon shirts and were peeling around the bottoms, showing white underneath. Hardin remembered a girl he had sneaked into one of these cabins one Friday night after a high school football game and done not quite the whole thing with.

He got out of the car slowly, on account of his knee. The parking lot was dried clay with different sizes of gravel in it, but it felt almost liquid under his feet. Come a chip floater, he thought with one part of his brain, come a real frog choker, it would be. He was wondering what his mother might really have been like, why she left them, if not for another man.

He supposed number three belonged to the Oldsmobile. The number had been taken off the door, unscrewed and pried out of the layers of different-colored paint, leaving a ragged three-shaped impression. He knocked, feeling a terrific impulse to ask his father what had really happened. A car, then another, swished by on the road. At the sound of a truck he turned his head: it was a big reefer, probably bound for one of the supermarkets. He knocked again.

The door opened suddenly against the chain bolt, and the muzzle of the pistol appeared beneath a slice of his father's face: one bloodhound eye, a strip of gullied cheek, a corner of the suspicious mouth, a section of the sharp jaw where the skin sagged off it. What an old man he is, Hardin thought, with a kind of surprise.

"Oh," Maynard said in the dismissive manner he always took towards his grown sons, "it's you." He closed the door and rattled around with the chain bolt, while Hardin stood there, his impulse to ask gone, knowing perfectly well he had already heard anything his father would say on the subject.

Maynard let him in without welcome or surprise. The cabins were darker and lower-ceilinged than Hardin remembered, and this one had a mildewed smell. An empty pint bottle of Jim Beam sat on the nightstand. The hollowed-out bed was wrinkled but still made up, and his father had obviously slept in his clothes. His tooled cowboy belt with the big buckle hung over a chair; his boots lay splayed on their sides. He had not started to dress like a cowboy until he had become a real estate broker. He stood there, rubbing a baggy eye with a fist, still holding the pistol down at his side. His dark gray hair stood up in a peak like a rooster comb on one side.

There was a television set on the desk or dresser, and Hardin figured he could knock his father into the screen before he had time to raise the pistol, but this was merely by way of scoping out the situation. Hardin did not want to hit his father. He did not even think he could beat the truth out of him. The truth, Hardin thought from somewhere, was not in him.

Hardin said to his father, "Give me the gun," and held out his callused left palm.

His father looked surprised, then looked at the thing as if he'd just found it at the end of his arm. With a gesture that said he could not imagine why anybody would be interested in it, he laid it in Hardin's hand, but Hardin had an idea his father was glad to get rid of it. The ease of all this shook Hardin a bit, and he did not know what to do next.

"Now listen here," he blustered. He did not know what he was going to say, and he thought at the same time that he was never going to know what had really happened between his parents, even if he went and asked that woman, his mother, because what would she tell him?

His father peered at him as if through knotholes. Then his face bunched up like a child's. "She, she . . . ." His father meant Dixie, and Hardin thought of bright Dixie, going on.

"You know that's not true," he said. And though he doubted his father knew any such thing, Maynard seemed willing to take Hardin's word for it. He bent stiffly from the hips on account of his bad back and sat down on the corner of the bed. Something seemed to've shifted from one to the other of them.

Then Hardin thought of what he wanted to say to his father, not that he believed it mattered to his father what he said, or whether he said anything. His father was sitting, head in hand, with his elbow on his knee, so that Hardin spoke to the back of his wrinkled neck.

"We don't do that kind of thing," Hardin said firmly, though he knew they always had. It was just the kind of thing they always had done.

Coming into Rio Harbor

After we got home and called the police, we sat in the room they called the library drinking gin and trying to get hold of ourselves, while the light dimmed out of the room little by little. The room was full of expensive replicas of antique lamps, but we didn't turn any of them on, and the last things I could see in the room before it went dark were the gold frame on Augustus John's portrait of Goedele hanging over the fireplace and the white flowers in the red-and-white twenties dress she was painted in. Julian called her the Love of My Life. She'd been dead for thirty years. The time Lottie told me this, I said Julian would have to have a love of his life.

"Yes," Lottie said in her staccato way, "if not her, then someone else. And she would have to be dead."

"And painted by Augustus John, and hanging over some beautiful mantelpiece."

"Or maybe her heart preserved in formaldehyde," Lottie said, "in crystal. Waterford. Or her whole self, like Lenin." We laughed.

But afterwards Lottie said more thoughtfully, "It is easy, is it not, to love the dead? And yet, he does love her, or he believes he does."

IN MEMORIAM—Hamill, Frankie, d. 17 April 1972, five years ago today (suddenly, as the result of an explosion). Gone but not forgotten. Our dead live on in our ideals.
> We will not give up
> That for which you died.
> In Jesus' name, Mother-in-law and Family.
> (*Londonderry News*, 18 April 1977)

Lottie had lived with him for three years, ready to leave him for half that time. "He is a monster," she said once: but this is the way Lottie talks. "And yet, there is something about him. Why do you think I am still here? It is not only because I do not want to spend all my days in some office. There are other men with money."

When I met her, she was sprawled out on a light-colored hearthrug in a black dress in the drawing room of a less remote Irish country house. I was the visiting American, invited by slight acquaintance, gawking. Very chic, very European, she looked Greek, had lived in Greece for years; her first husband had been a Greek. In fact, she was German—a remote cousin of Heinrich Himmler ("Well, it's not my fault!" she said). She told me all this in our first conversation. How near the end of the war her father, who was a commercial butcher, had resigned from the Nazi party and been drafted into the army and sent to the Russian front, where he was killed. How her sisters had emigrated to the States, and she'd once lived in New York for a year herself.

We were friends immediately. "Oh, you must come north for Christmas!" she said, and she meant it.

Julian said, "Oh, yes, do." He smiled, his lips pressed together. Maybe sixty years old, maybe forty pounds overweight, he sat tightly on a small straight chair in a black three-piece suit, with the waistcoat cut very high over the tie.

That same evening, we also met Mick Jagger. I didn't recognize him. I said, "Oh, and what do you do?"

He said, "I'm a rock and roll singer." He had on a Mickey Mouse T-shirt and a diamond.

"Well," the woman said, "'twas the only place I could find, but as you see, it's not good. There's no place for the children to play except in the street, with the soldiers walking up and down. And although the building was put up only four years ago, there's big chunks of plaster falling, and down the hall is always overflowing, and of course, the two wee rooms is not enough for the nine of us.

"After I pay the rent and the electric, I have usually about four pounds left for the week. With that I buy usually bread, margarine, tea, sugar, the powdered milk, and some eggs. Sometimes I buy cabbage and a small bit of bacon instead of the eggs. When Brian was working and, of course, we had more—not a great deal, but a bit more—I would do the shopping every day. And in those days I would sometimes buy rashers and potatoes and things. But now I usually go right out and spend the money on bread all at once, so that we will have it.

"It's a bad dream I have at times—that the children will starve. This way, I give the children a slice in the morning and two slices for tea, except sometimes towards the end of the week there's only one slice for tea. We always eat up the eggs right away, and if I let the children drink any of the powdered milk, we'd have none for the tea half the week.

"Ach, I don't know. Things couldn't go on the way they were. One side of the community had all the jobs and the other side had none. Brian worked with those people, and he always said that they were the best people in the world. I just don't know what it is. I guess they've never gotten close enough to us. They regard us as monsters.

"I couldn't say. You mean, do they think that if we have a bit more, it's the less for them? The dear Lord knows we've all little enough."

(A.-L. Mahier, Women of the World, 1977)

Tourists among the rich, we were intrigued at how Julian had come by his wealth, or appearance of wealth, as it seemed now mostly to be. "Oh, people gave him money," Lottie said as we drove past his wintering green fields. "He acts as if he had inherited stacks and stacks of money, but he has got this all," she waved her hand, "by simply assuming that he deserves it."

She turned into the drive and the grocery sacks shifted across the back seat. Out there in the country, miles from everything, we had to cross the border to shop. It was the Wednesday before Christmas, and the next Sunday the grocer's where we had been was blown up. They were after somebody who lived upstairs, we heard. From the bridge, where we waited in the inevitable rain while Welsh soldiers checked IDs, we could see the steel beams of what had been the custom house drawn up at one corner in the shape of a flame.

"A sort of con-man, then," I said.

"Oh, no," she said. "People gave to him because they loved him. Look at me if you doubt that."

She kept the great house for him, managed the farm—in New York, she had managed a medium-sized hotel. They were breeding cattle, but he took no interest in it; she and the farm man did everything. And she shopped and cooked and cleaned, had people over—Julian's social acquaintances, who had become her own—or gave parties for them. She was introduced around the county as his companion.

"And they all think they know," she said. "Isn't it funny?"

They were not lovers. "Oh, I think it stopped around six months after I got here. I don't care who knows. It had been all right, not great, but you see I was so much in love with him I didn't care, and then one night he said, 'Get the clothes brush,' and he started beating me with it, and I said no, and he said, 'Well, I have to have something more,' and I said, 'Well, not that, because it hurts and I don't like it.'

"And that was it," she said. "Except for one time, I think."

The house was one of those square eighteenth-century jobs you used to see all over Ireland with the roof caved in, which was the way Julian had bought it. He had fixed it up with his third wife's money. There were gilt birds at the tops of the rainspouts—also floodlights he'd put in just the year before, Lottie said, for security.

"Julian is no different from many others," Lottie said, "and in his charm as well. He had nothing to start with and he was nobody in particular."

Perhaps that was part of our fascination with him, that he

had once been as we were. And yet, we did not think we would've done what he had to get where he was.

"I have heard him say, 'My father spent everything he had to send me to school at Rugby.' Because for them, that is everything." She waved her hand in the pigskin glove. "They were rather ordinary upper-middle class English people.

"His father had some kind of successful and, you know, what they regard as more or less acceptable business—the wine trade, or something—but there was no aristocracy at all. Except the Portuguese great-grandfather. You will notice that is the only one of his relatives he ever talks about." This was the great-grandfather who had received a peerage and an estate from the emperor and empress of Brazil for helping restore them to the throne of Portugal.

Lottie drove slowly up the rough farm drive, her gloved hands loosely on the wheel of the Mini. "I think it was some famous old London queen—though Julian was not that way— who got him into it, what we would call now the international jet set—a man who was in love with Julian when he was young. He was terribly good-looking, you know. He was in a movie, I do not think a very good one.

"All his wives had money, and the duchess who was his mistress, whom he still calls his friend, once gave him forty thousand pounds to invest in something. Of course, he later sold out of it for I don't know how many times as much.

"And Goedele, of course," the love of his life who killed herself in Rio de Janeiro, "left him everything. Not that she had much by then."

From the kitchen steps the dogs ran out at the car.

"Go on! Get out of the way! Oh, yes, that is true. He has her silver. I have seen it in the vault in London. Of course, whatever he had once, he is going broke from the boat."

The boat was the yacht he was building to sail to Brazil in the summer. "He will have a hundred-thousand-pound mortgage on it before he is through," Lottie said. "I don't know why they give it to him. He says, 'I must have it,' and they give it to him. He is quite mad; he does not care about his debts. You have to realize . . . ," Lottie stopped. "Oh, these people: it is all a matter of class."

> Now reptilian armored cars rumble through the streets. Barbed wire and road blocks bar every roadway into the bomb-devastated ghost town of the city center. Troops in blackface patrol the neighborhood like a jungle of a foreign land.
>
> (Jordan Bonaparte, "In Londonderry, Tragedy Touches a Man of Peace," *Life*, August 18, 1972)

From where we sat in the car, we could see fields just across the river, in Northern Ireland, and far mountains in the distance. The engine ticked, cooling in the quiet. In a moment we would unpack the car, carry groceries inside. What happened to Goedele, I wanted to know.

"Oh, it is quite a story," Lottie said, turning her square shoulders, her high-boned olive face to me. "She was the wife of some East Prussian nobleman who sent her to Berlin when the Russians advanced, and stayed behind. 'My house, my furniture, my art collections. Without these things, my life would not be my life.' He was captured and died in a concentration camp. He was much older than she was. It is all in her memoirs. There is a copy in the library. Then she met Julian in Berlin after the war. He was a naval attaché, still a young man; she was a middle-aged woman.

"They had gone to Rio together; one wonders how, as neither of them had any money. Apparently it was quite the place after the war, and perhaps he meant to take her to where he, too, had pretensions of aristocracy. They had a quarrel. He went out. When he came back she was dead, in the hotel room, of sleeping pills. Who knows why? But, you know, he said to me quite recently, and he does not talk about her, she had lived through so much already. Life as she had known it was over. I think she is on his mind nowadays. Perhaps it is the trip to Rio, or this other war."

This other war was never very far away. Locking the garage, Lottie said, "We never used to lock things up, but since Gordon was killed last Christmas . . . In his car, with a bullet in his head. They found him the next day. A very prominent businessman. Not involved in politics. Insofar as anybody is not."

Out there in the country, with the wind blowing, the silence of the house was loud, and Julian sat away downstairs in his study over plans for his yacht all day and sometimes all night. Lottie lowered her voice in the kitchen, "They should kill him, you know." She was taking groceries out of the sacks, still wearing her coat and gloves. "You are shocked, but they should kill all of the ones like him, strictly speaking. If anybody was running this war properly, which they are not."

They buried Agnes McAnoy, 62, widow and mother of three, in Belfast last week. And Molly McAleavy, 57, mother of eleven. And Marie Bennett, 42, mother of seven. And Arthur Penn, 33, father of three. And Elizabeth Carson, 64, whose husband Willy lost an arm. Pathetic lines of mourners wept after the requiem at the Catholic Church of St. Matthew, half a mile from where the attackers had tossed a bomb into the crowded Strand Bar in East Belfast.

(*Time*, April 28, 1975)

The rest, all Protestants, were then gunned down in a withering hail of automatic fire. Ten died instantly. At week's end the badly wounded survivor remained in serious condition at a nearby hospital. The killings are believed to have been carried out in retaliation for the assassination the previous night of five Catholics.

(*Time*, January 19, 1976)

All Julian seemed interested in was the yacht—the yacht and the Atlantic crossing to Rio that he was going to make as soon as it was finished. He had lived there for a while, after the war: his second wife had been a Brazilian girl.

"She was very rich and very young," Lottie said, "and he spent all her money and divorced her." They had been divorced for sixteen years. He was still friendly with her, though. "He has to be," Lottie said. "He owes her alimony he has never paid."

She showed up for Christmas, too. She telephoned from London, where she lived, two days before. On the telephone in the hall, Julian made a face. "Why yes, Lina," he said, "do come. That would be lovely."

Afterwards he said, as if to himself, "It won't be so bad having her, with the others." The others were me and a gray man, an old friend of Julian's who was the descendant of a famous British military hero.

"Ah, it's just like old times again," Lina said, coming in the front door with her chin in the air, though she had never lived in that house. She was a plain-looking, middle-aged woman with a wide nose and red-dyed hair.

Lottie and I wanted to sympathize with her for what Julian had done to her. "She works at a travel agency," Lottie said. "She has to. She has nothing."

She did seem to have a lot of clothes. She kept changing into different outfits several times a day. She cried over her Christmas present from Julian ("Oh, darling," she said to him). It was a book about cats, which Lottie had bought "because I am sure he has not thought of her."

We all met at meals in the dining room, where the wallpaper was supposed to represent Brazil: Julian had had it printed up from eighteenth-century plates in the Victorian and Albert Museum. On one wall black-booted conquistadores discharged a volley from blunderbusses at naked brown Indians fitting arrows into bows behind brilliant green palm fronds; on another, white-shirted overseers with whips stood over black slaves cutting cane. A jaguar crouched in the jungle under a boa constrictor, while gauchos in red neckerchiefs twirled lassos on the pampas and the mountains towered lavender round blue Rio Harbor.

Julian and the gray man discussed British military history. When Lina mentioned her psychoanalysis, everybody looked away, and she talked about her cats instead.

She stayed for three days, until she and Julian had a fight in the middle of the night, and he drove her to Belfast airport at four o'clock one morning.

"Like everyone else," says shipyard worker John Bleakley, "we stay at home at night with our own kind and don't answer the door."
(*Time*, September 11, 1972)

For the last few weeks, we rarely saw Julian except at mealtimes. He would come up from the study, where he sat all day at his desk in front of the framed proclamation of thanks from the emperor and empress of Brazil to his great-grandfather. There he busied himself with minor decisions about the yacht.

That midday he paused, abstracted, in the doorway of the dining room, his face the color of the burgundy he drank afternoons and evenings, his mind still on what he had been thinking about. He had on a pair of old woolen suit trousers with a small hole above the knee and a raveling sweater. You could see he had once been good-looking; he still acted like a man who is good-looking. "But I think he has stopped caring about it," Lottie said another time. "It is a matter of habit."

We had been standing in the dining room waiting for him. He looked from one of us to the other and said, "Do you think the bottom color should be painted only up to the waterline, or eighteen inches above it?"

Lottie made a noise with her mouth and did not say anything.

At the sideboard, Julian uncorked a bottle of wine. He had small hands, with the little fingers so curved they looked almost deformed. "Always have green glasses for white wine," he said to nobody in particular.

When he had sat down at the table and surveyed what was offered, he raised an eyebrow. "Omelet. Don't much like eggs myself. They eat a lot of eggs in this country."

"The price of meat!" said Lottie, who tried to run the household economically.

"They eat a lot of eggs in this country," he repeated, picking up his fork. "They like 'em."

The meal was not much different from any other we three had shared alone. Julian made an effort at polite conversation but seemed bored by it. We talked, as we often had, about politics and the war, which he believed to be a manifestation of the inherent savagery of the Irish. Towards the end of the meal we were talking about salmon fishing rights on the river: there had just been something about that on the TV news.

"They want to make extra money," he said, "and poaching is easier than working at whatever it is they do. It's as simple as that." He began to peel a banana with a knife and fork. He regarded the ability to do this as a test of civilized table manners.

"But there is no work for them," Lottie said. "How are they to support their families?"

"If they'd stop blowing up businesses, there'd be work." ("There was *never* work!" Lottie said. "That is why—")

"And why should they have families at all?" Julian said.

Lottie made some gesture to indicate that this was too silly a question to reply to. "He calls himself a liberal," she said to me privately, after some earlier one of these discussions.

"Well, of course," he went on, "I understand that they *will* have families. But why should they? You've seen their wretched children.

"Look here," he said, as if to set things straight on the subject once and for all. "The salmon fishing rights have been awarded by government contract to the company, and anyone else who fishes the river for salmon is stealing. They ought to put armed men out there. That would stop it, provide work, too. Except, of course, you couldn't hire one of them who wouldn't sell out to his friends."

"What is the matter with you?" Lottie said. "One would think, to listen to you, that you had no sense at all!"

Julian merely gave her an amused glance and ate his banana with knife and fork. But afterwards, as if he thought this would placate her, he said, "My dear, I wonder if you would come downstairs this afternoon and give me your opinion about some things on the yacht."

"The yacht! The yacht!" she raved. "If I hear one more thing about that yacht, I shall lose my mind, like you!" By the time she was through with this, though, she seemed to have used up her anger.

"You're tired," he said kindly.

She admitted she hadn't slept well the night before. "Take a nap," he said.

"If I take a nap I won't sleep tonight either," she grumbled.

"Mm. Don't sleep much myself these days." He mused briefly.

"I'll tell you. Why don't we all go for a drive?" He looked from her to me, me to her.

We didn't say anything; she and I had driven all over the North and West of Ireland together and thought the roads belonged to us. We did not especially want to spend the afternoon driving around with him.

To me, he said, "Have you seen Grianan Aileach?" This was an ancient ring fort that he knew I wanted to see.

"I've seen it a hundred times," Lottie said.

"Oh, but Debra wants to see it," he said. "We must go to Grianan Aileach."

And so we went out that afternoon, by his choice and because of who we all were.

In the last chapter the man identified pseudonymously as Peter McHare makes the following confession: "When, according to our orders, we arrived at the house, I remembered being there once as a boy. The man bred dogs on the side, and my father or one of his friends had gone there twenty years before concerning the purchase of a dog.

"When Michael told him he was under arrest and we had orders to bring him to trial, the prisoner said (or words to this effect), 'Then if I'm to be tried in a court of law, you'll not mind if I ring up my lawyer.'

"Michael said that was regrettably not possible, that under the new order full legal process would be restored, but the exigencies of war made such impossible now.

"We took him away under the eyes of his wife and child. The prisoner was tried by military tribunal and, as the major shareholder in Harmon Dee, Ltd., Linenweavers, found guilty of having for many years consumed the people's substance.

"Asked if he had anything to say for himself the prisoner said that he had lived according to the order of things as he found them, and that it had not occurred to him to think that he did wrong. The prisoner was known about the neighborhood for a good-tempered man and an honest breeder of Irish wolfhounds, and his reputation was brought out in his defense.

"He was sentenced to death by firing squad, and we were ordered to carry out the sentence, the trial taking approximately ten minutes.

"After the kerchief was around his eyes, he was given the opportunity to say whatever he had to say, and these are his exact words: 'I wish to convey my love to my wife Charlotte and to our son and daughter; I beg pardon of all whom I have offended; and I commend my soul to its Maker.'

"The order being given, the execution was carried out. Our men standing by were affected by the prisoner's behavior, and, it may be to put heart into the rest of us, the officer second in command said that though shocking things might be done to improve the people's lot, he would do them himself, since shocking things had always been done and, like as not, for bad reasons or no reasons at all.

"Exactly how they fixed on that man, out of many they might have chosen, I couldn't say."

("Review: *Peter McHare's Confession*," *Lately*, 7 August 1976)

Julian was particularly courteous and attentive, opening the car doors for us, seeing us in. He was handsome in a sheepskin coat with the collar turned up: his profile was still fine, above the chin. He drove north along the river and then on up into the mountains, being charming, pointing out things in the landscape with slight gestures. At every farm a black-and-white dog ran out at the car or sat watching us go by. At one farm the dog lay on top of a tall stone pillar.

"It's the same dog," Julian said. "Don't you think? How does he get from one place to the next so fast?"

The climbing road grew rough and finally ended. Above, on the summit, the round fort sat like a fez. We got out, climbed towards it, and went in the narrow passage through the thick unmortared wall. Inside, paper trash had been blown around a large grassy circle open to the sky. We climbed on up the ancient stacked-stone staircase that ran, narrow but utterly solid, around the inside of the wall.

"How they fit these stones together," Lottie said, "to last so long!"

"Sixth century," Julian said, "or seventh."

The wind at the top blew strong. "Warm enough?" Julian said "Lottie? Debra?"

The lesser mountains, blue where we looked up from the farm, were brown to look down on, with white roads snaking around them. Lough Swilly lay on one side, Lough Foyle on the other.

"This is where the flight of the earls took place," Julian said. "When Queen Elizabeth the First finally subdued the country. They drove them up this far, and down there from some harbor on Lough Swilly they took ship for Spain. The remnants of their aristocracy."

Over from Limavady, the pink smoke from the plastics factory spread out across a small patch of sky.

"There was still some history left when this thing was built," he mused. "Still some civilization to come. The English brought everything worthwhile to Ireland she ever had. Now it's falling apart."

Lottie said, "What's falling apart? Nothing's falling apart."

"Well, what do you call it?" He stretched his chin up and looked down at her. "People being murdered in their beds. The Bogside taking over."

And so the delusory peace was broken, but the outing seemed to be over, anyway. We had seen what there was to see. Julian went down the hill apart from us, having done his polite duty.

Back in the car, he slumped over the wheel and let us climb in by ourselves. Before he started the car, he said to Lottie, "You will look over those plans with me now, won't you?"

She sent me back a glance that said, "You see? He only did that so I will do what he wanted to begin with."

Early in October a number of women, whose husbands and sons were among the internees, broke down the outer

defenses of Long Kesh, surged into the compound and
burned several buildings.

(A. Boyd, "Imprisonment Without Trial," *Nation*,
November 30, 1974)

The valley where we came down was flat but with scattered
clumps of trees. So it was possible to drive, as we did, around
a tight curve and come suddenly on something we had had no
warning of in advance. There, at one of the British Army check-
points that had been empty all spring, a blue car was parked
crosswise, blocking the road.

"Oh, my God," Lottie said.

Two men in the back seat watched us over their shoulders
without moving. Julian put the Bentley in reverse, but already
there was another car blocking the road behind us.

"Where the *hell* did they come from?" Lottie whispered.

Julian said, "I always meant to put the revolver in the car."

And it's just as everyone says: you don't believe these things
will happen to you—at most, to someone you know slightly.
After the first flooding physical sensation of terror, my first
thought was, they shouldn't kill me, I'm a foreigner. Then I
thought, except that I will have seen them. Afterwards, Lottie
said she thought exactly the same things.

The driver from the car behind us got out and walked towards us, while another man was still struggling to get out. All
of this seemed to happen very slowly, but there was nothing
we could do. Then there were two men walking towards us,
and I saw that the man who had struggled to get out of the car
wore the right sleeve of his raincoat empty. He has lost an arm,
I thought at first; then I saw he held it inside the raincoat,
which he had buttoned up over something large.

When the driver, who was a young man, got up close
enough to look at Julian, he said, "It's not him." He wore an
old suit jacket that he kept his right hand in the pocket of.

He put his face right up to the open window on Julian's

side. He had straight shiny clean brown hair. "This is not the man," he said again.

The man with the bulky raincoat came up to the car and laughed in a funny way. "It is not. No, of course it is not." He was older and very Irish-looking, and he had the creases in his face of a man who smiled a lot, but he looked worried and irritated then.

The younger man called to the car up ahead, "This is not the man." Two men got out and came towards us, spare, hard-faced countrymen carrying unconcealed automatic rifles, which they pointed at us the rest of the time.

And then, when Lottie and I had tensely begun to hope, Julian said, "Tell your friends to get their car off the road."

Lottie drew a hissing breath through her teeth, and the older man, who seemed to be in charge, looked at Julian and turned away from the car. ("Will you shut *up*?" Lottie whispered to Julian.) He smiled at her coldly with his lips pressed together.

"It's the Bentley," one of the riflemen called back.

"As if there's not more than one Bentley in the county," the older man muttered, but not loud.

Julian stuck his head out the window and said to the two with the rifles, "Get your car off the road."

The older man in charge turned back towards Julian and asked in a casual sort of way, "And who might you be?"

"I am Julian Powell-deBarros of Foyle House," he said, "and you are blocking a public road."

The older man seemed to have a tic around the eyes that Julian's saying this set off. His face twitched, and he turned away again. The other men had drawn together in a little group, and he went to join them. They eyed us and seemed to argue. ("You have got us all killed!" Lottie whispered to Julian.)

After a few minutes, the group broke up and all four men came towards us, the two with the automatic rifles in the lead this time. One of them said to Julian, "Aye, you'll do."

The older man gestured ridiculously with the thing he had been holding buttoned up inside his raincoat, and the muzzle of a large weapon stuck out. "Now, if you'll just come quietly with us."

"Bandits!" Julian said, but he got out of the car.

"Now, Miss," the man leaned on the car and put his head up to the window, "you drive."

Later Lottie said to me, "They feel very secure. These things are never prosecuted. Everyone is afraid."

She slid over into the driver's seat and looked at the man. "Let him go with us," she pleaded. "He's half-mad. He's not responsible." The man looked away into the distance and his face twitched.

"Of course I'm responsible," Julian said; it was not clear who he was speaking to. "And so are these men, all of them."

The man looked back into the car. "Now, ladies, you'd best drive straight home," he said. Then the road ahead was open, and Lottie put the car in gear.

The last look we had of Julian, he was standing there very erect, smiling a little with satisfaction, as if at least it was all happening the way he knew it should be.

We drove back to the house and called the police, where Lottie was a long time making them understand what had happened.

> I have hated God's enemies with a perfect hate.
> (The Rev. Ian Paisley)

We huddled in the cold library waiting for the police, who would not be able to do anything, clutching the heavy square glasses. At first Lottie had busied herself with ice cubes, the ice bucket, as if for some ordinary social visit; then she said, "What am I doing?" and we just sat.

"It is frightening," she said at one point, "when things happen after you have said they should."

We felt, too, the guilt of being alive.

"Maybe they'll let him go," I said, though I didn't believe it, "or he'll get away. Maybe they'll demand ransom."

"No," Lottie said.

After a while, she said, "He was the one who wanted to go out."

Later she said, "And always, he must act the master."

Then we were silent for a long time, while the room got dark.

After I couldn't even see her sitting at the other end of the long tweed sofa, she said in a different tone, "I suppose he does not mind much—did not. Would even prefer it to a heart attack. When I first knew him, he used to say that when he was old he was going to live at the Ritz in London, have a room on the Green Park side, and never go out at all, make people come and visit him if they wanted to see him. But it had been a long time even then since he had the money to do a thing like that."

She was silent again, and we sat on in that eerie evening feeling of an empty house where the lights have not yet been turned on. Minutes passed, five, ten.

She burst out: "He says, 'Civilization is on the decline everywhere,' but he is, was, talking about himself. He had only his fifty-nine-year-old collapsing body and his life in the grand style, which is a what-do-you-call-it—completely out of date in the modern world. I do not think there was anything for him beyond the yacht and the trip to Rio."

Then she was quiet again.

In the end she said, "You know what it was about him that attracted me, long after I ceased to care for him in other ways? It was that he believed in himself. It's like he used to say to me sometimes, grab hold of me and say to me—even in these last months when we've meant very little to each other—'I love you, I need you, you know that, don't you?'

"And it wasn't true. Not the way you or I would think of love. But it was true to him. Whatever rot he talked, whatever wrong he did, he never questioned. He believed that it was right."

I said whoever heard of such a thing.

"Oh, well, yes, of course," she said, "and especially the people around here."

"Not us?" I said.

She said, "That is different."

"I suppose they all think that."

"Then they are wrong!" she said, and we laughed, from the strain, and got up and turned on the lights.

All Dance

I never even met the woman, but I'll be lying in bed happy with my lover, and suddenly I'll think of her, Beatrice. I'll remember, as if I'd lived them myself, things the Colonel, who was never my lover, told me about her. The Colonel and I had our own brief flirtation—it was what he came to afterwards— but though he was attractive in a red-faced, white-haired sort of way and terrifically kind, we were not each other's type, a generation apart. Like Beatrice, he was Patti Page, Frank Sinatra, Guy Lombardo to my Stones, Doors, Tina. I'd hoped to teach the Colonel to boogie, before I knew him well, but to him, all that shaking around just looked ridiculous. The Colonel, who liked to know what was what, danced only organized dances—the waltz, fox-trot, polka, cha-cha.

It was dancing that he met Beatrice, at the Starlight Seniors' Ballroom Club, an organization of which he was president. Actually, being retired and a widower, he was president of a lot of things. He did not particularly like dancing, though perhaps he liked the opportunity to embrace women he was otherwise separated from by the customs of their generation. I don't mean he thought about it that way, or at all.

I went with him to the SSBC a few times. So when I think of him meeting Beatrice there, I imagine how he turns away from talking to some people—always talking to some people, the Colonel—and catches sight of her as she stands up on a shore of red-draped tables across the cavernous ballroom. A wide-lipped Scandinavian-looking blond, late fifties, early sixties, with a serene, grand carriage, a woman who carries her size proudly, like a yacht. She is splendid, monumental. The Colonel has never seen her before, and he knows practically everybody in the SSBC.

He cuts rapidly across the red carpet, onto the dance floor, towards her. A waltz is upcoming, from Gene McCown and the Big Band Sound.

But by the time the Colonel has wound his way among the standing groups and couples and presented himself before

135

her, she has already promised the waltz—to a slim sleek character named Mr. Turrentine, say, who sells shoes the rest of the week and is known in the SSBC for his showy, exhibition style of dancing.

"Ah," says the Colonel, looking up from Beatrice down to her partner, beaming redly, as if at all their good fortunes. He himself is middling height and thickish, and since his retirement has never put on anything dressier than a pair of chinos and a golf shirt.

To Beatrice I give a black dress—the ladies of the SSBC go dressed up on Tuesday nights—with a sort of latticework over her freckled bosom, not a new dress but a nice dress, such as she might've worn on special occasions for years. The Colonel notices her pale gold-and-silver hair because it seems too tightly cropped for her, short back and sides, but he guesses they're wearing it that way nowadays. Punkish.

"Then perhaps," he says in the memory that is not really mine at all, "I might have the honor of the next dance? Unless it's a tango." The Colonel does not tango.

And I can see the utterly confident smile of self-deprecation he would've bestowed on Mr. Turrentine, who does, of course, tango but whose elevated, whose *dancing* expression might be baked on for all it ever changes.

Beatrice smiles her own slow wide-lipped smile. She says she will have to rest after the waltz but "maybe later."

The Colonel assents heartily, "By all means, by all means," and, with a thick and hairy forearm, hands Beatrice to Mr. Turrentine as if she were his own before grabbing the nearest powdery gray lady and rotating her into the waltz.

In my few times at the SSBC, I did learn to waltz and to foxtrot, being myself open to all the possibilities of dancing, but I always felt a little silly mincing along backwards like that. Still, though the SSBC is not my scene, it is a scene. Gray-haired widows and divorcees in pairs and groups, hoping for a dance as if it might be something more (though it is always only a dance); here and there the lone male counterpart, preening a little in his gameness; and the couples, the serious ballroom performers, showing off their wiry live limbs and hot steps. An aura of significance about it all—or so it seemed to me— entirely missing from the free frolic of rock and roll.

Later the Colonel danced with Beatrice, talked to her. She told him she had come to the SSBC because she did not think she had danced enough in her life. She told him—I see her gesture to a group at a table—that she had come with friends.

And I see the pair of them sit down at an empty red-draped table, on which there is a red glass jar covered with white plastic fishnet. Perhaps Beatrice tilts the candle-holder towards her and says in her deliberate way, "This one is not lit," and the Colonel produces matches and lights it without noticing what he is doing. He is noticing the freckles on her arm, her blunt worn hand holding the jar. She is pleased by the glow of the candle.

She tells him she has a son, thirty-five, and a daughter, thirty-three, both living at home now. The Colonel and his wife never had children. She tells him she is "alone"—she does not say whether widowed or divorced. She sits beautifully up-right, and he is moved by the unself-conscious dignity of her large body.

By the time she says she is tired and must leave, the Colonel has written down her telephone number in a little book among those of his many other friends and acquaintances.

He calls her up to ask her out, and she accepts his invitation with such grave and innocent delight that he guesses she has not been taken out much. Picking her up at the tan brick house on the unfashionable south side of town is a little awkward, because of the bumptious, beer-gutted son sitting in the living room watching television. But the son has, after all, Beatrice's beautiful lips, and the Colonel's nuclear charm is equal to all confrontations. And they have a wonderful time.

The Colonel takes Beatrice out several more times, to dinner, to movies, to Tuesday nights at the SSBC. He meets the
tall, sturdy-looking daughter, who has recently come back to
live with her mother after separating from her own husband
but who at least has a respectable job. (The son, on the other
hand, has never left home, apparently never done much of
anything in life except sit in the living room watching television.) The Colonel finds out that Beatrice is not widowed but
long divorced, that she reared her children alone, that she
worked until recently for her brother, an insurance broker.
The Colonel also has the sense of not finding out a lot of things
about Beatrice. There is a reserve about her. She will take
some time to get to know, he thinks.

But this does not keep him from beginning to fall for her.
He has been widowed two or three years and is, after all, ripe.
He has been cultivated with casseroles and blandished with
propositions; he has a large acquaintance of widows and divorcees, and he believes he knows what is out there. He feels
affected by Beatrice as he has felt by no one else. He is warmed
by the thought of her large body beneath its armor of foundation garments, and he is intrigued by her. So far, he has only
kissed her lightly, a few social smacks. But he has begun to
entertain disconnected bright flashes in his mind, of her rich
curves between strange sheets; breakfast in a flowery courtyard in some tropical country; the two of them getting off a
tour bus in an ornate gray city in what he understands to be
Europe. Married? Honeymooning? Why not, he thinks.

Then one afternoon she invites him over for a cup of coffee,
and I imagine that they are sitting in what she calls the garden
room of her house. There was such a room, a window-walled
addition, perhaps dark all the same in the winter afternoon,
under the large old trees of the side yard. And for some reason
I see this room furnished with sofa and chairs whose curved
blond arms are all in the shape of half wagon wheels, a blond

coffee table like a whole wagon wheel laid flat, covered with glass. Anyhow, Beatrice would not have chosen the living room, where the son was, for so private a talk.

"I must tell you," she says, fixing her light-lashed eyes on the Colonel firmly. And then she tells him she has cancer. Oh, very dispassionately, she tells him. How she had it before, a few years back, and the doctors thought they had gotten it. "And then, in the fall," she says. She has freckles on her arms and on her high round forehead that run together, and perhaps the Colonel cannot pull his attention away from these, so that it seems to him he cannot properly concentrate on what she is saying, what he is saying back to her.

But the Colonel volunteers four mornings a week at St. Agnes' Hospital, indeed is chief of volunteers there, and he is familiar with the ordeal of cancer patients. So he does say the right things, ask the questions.

"No," she says at one point, thank God, she will have no more chemo.

"I'll live part of this year," she says serenely. Not—she smiles her beautiful smile—that the doctors put it quite that way. "They said, the doctor said, that if there were things I had always wanted to do . . ." That was why she started going to the SSBC, she explains. Her arm, alive and warm, rests on the curved blond wood of the sofa arm.

And the Colonal saw again his scattered bright hopes, now never to be gathered together into anything.

Then or another time Beatrice points out the redwood bird-feeder she hung, "after I found that out," from a low limb of some wide old live oak in the yard. That was another thing she wanted to do: see more birds. Even as she says that, I see a flock of cedar waxwings move in, flashing their yellow breasts among the firethorn, seizing the berries with never a thought about whether they ought to.

It was all very sad, this projected death of hers. Still, she had come to terms with it by then, and it was hers.

But the Colonel—he is brusque as he leaves that afternoon, as near to unkind as he will ever be to her. I imagine him driving home in the failing light in his late-model cream-colored Oldsmobile, letting himself in from the big double garage to the big empty suburban house he and his wife had bought for their retirement shortly before she died. He feels something of what he did then: that particular injustice of death which consists of its terrible timing. I see him putting a Hungry Man Southern Dinner in the microwave, poking at the steaming corn bread with a stubby finger, eating nothing. I see him padding around the carpeted house in his bathrobe and slippers, waking early and fretting until the sky begins to lighten and he can go out and vacuum up a few more of the big papery sycamore leaves off his lawn that have blown over from the neighbors'. Afterwards he stands awhile staring absently at their yard, which does not seem to've been cleaned up since fall; then he thinks, what the hell, and goes over and makes a job of it.

At one point, he said, he was angry at Beatrice's calm acceptance of her death, her refusal even to regret the life she might've lived with him. At another point he believed there must be something he could do. He talked to her doctors at the hospital, but things were as she had said. It was a little like his wife, who had dropped dead one night of a heart attack while pouring herself a glass of milk. He had administered CPR, called the emergency wagon, all to no help. She must've been dead, a doctor he knew well told him later, by the time she hit the floor.

In the end, the Colonel accepted that Beatrice would die and he could not prevent it. But he retained an inclination to help out.

And so he began to do the kinds of things with and for Beatrice that she was already doing for herself—appointed himself, you might say, her personal hospice volunteer. The

Colonel, after all, volunteered at all kinds of things. The only thing unusual about his helping Beatrice was that he had been almost in love with her. Of course, he didn't feel the same about her by this time. He couldn't. Nevertheless, he commenced to try to provide Beatrice with whatever she thought would charm her remaining days and round out her life.

A lot of it was very romantic. Moonlight walks along the river, hot spiced cider in front of a fire afterwards. Late night dancing overlooking the city. Driving up Mount Mirabeau B. to watch the sunrise. Beatrice had not had much romance in her life.

Well, the Colonel could do romance. He knew it was something women liked, or at least the women his own age. (I'm not romantic myself, and I think this was one of the things the Colonel found a relief about me.) For himself, he could take it or leave it. But when the occasion required, he could believe in himself as rather a dashing fellow. So that, as Beatrice opens the door, there he is, standing on the doorstep of the tan brick house grinning, holding an enormous satin heartful of candy. Or again with the bunch of tiny yellow florist's roses in cellophane, as easily as if romance itself had been a kind of optional packaging. Of course, activities requiring Beatrice to do anything had to be carefully planned because she was not strong.

The Colonel helped her out, too, with some practical matters, which he understood better. She wanted to install a new gas range, for the children, he supposed, who would go on living in the house after she was gone. So the Colonel took her to Sears to pick one out, with a black glass oven door, and afterwards packed his red toolbox over to her house to connect it—the son, he guessed, would've just let it sit there. She wanted to plant a garden. So the Colonel spent several cold afternoons digging bags of sand and something sold as Well-Rotted Sheep Manure into a patch of the heavy black clay in her backyard, then watched her plant green peas and two kinds of lettuce and some spinach, while she chatted unself-consciously about where the hot-weather crops would go, the green beans and tomatoes and purple-hull peas.

She chatted on freely about a lot of things during these activities, as if the disclosure of her whole life to him had only had to wait on the disclosure of her death. She told him about her youth in a strict Swedish-American farming community and about how, when she was an adolescent during World War II, there had been a prisoner-of-war camp nearby for German prisoners, who had been put to work raising cotton, and how she had secretly watched them from across the fields with some intense emotion she did not know how to name. She told him, too, how she had married her husband, Arne, but after they had moved to Ft. Worth so he could work in a factory, he had left her to go to California. Though he had said he would send for her and the two children when he got work, she had not believed him at the time, and he never did. She never heard from him after that. Years later, when her family had persuaded her to get a divorce, they found out he was alive in California.

And yet, another time she declared that she had been fortunate in life, really. She had had family to help her when her husband left. She had moved here, gone to work for her brother in the insurance business; he had helped her buy the tan brick house. She had raised her children. She did not regret anything.

Then—I see her satisfied, after dinner in a restaurant, wearing that same black dress—she sighs at a different memory, leans a shoulder against the old limestone wall by the table and says, "Only some things about my marriage."

And though the Colonel, who has listened kindly to everything, pours her another glass of white wine, she doesn't say any more right then.

It's a few days later, after one of her household projects, when she tells him about this. I imagine her making coffee in her kitchen, the Colonel sitting on a plastic-covered chair at an old chrome-and-yellow kitchen table. Between pouring the water into the new drip machine and putting the coffee into the filter, she confesses that what she most regrets about her marriage is that she never enjoyed sex; she did not even know she was supposed to. But, she says, she has heard and read so much about it since "on television and in the magazines!" that she believes she understands now how it is supposed to be.

Then, just as if thinking out loud, and not at all as if she is suggesting it as something for them to do, she says this is something else she would like to experience before she dies.

For once, the Colonel truly doesn't know what to say, but apparently she doesn't expect him to say anything.

He sure thought about it afterwards, though. He hadn't expected that he would ever have sex with her, after she told him about her cancer. Not that he was turned off by the idea; he just hadn't thought she would do it without the kind of plans and promises they couldn't make. But, hey, he thought, if she wants to. And it pleased him to think that he could do this for her.

And so the next time he takes her home from an evening, as they stand in the dark of the front porch, he pulls her face down to his and kisses her, really kisses her. She returns his kisses with such enthusiasm that he goes on, mouth and hands as far as he can standing up fully dressed.

Soon he is looking out of the corner of his eye at the porch swing, or the wide concrete balustrade, but he thinks of the awkwardness for a woman who has never enjoyed sex before, and of her fragile condition. "Shall we go in and lie down?" he murmurs.

He thinks she is about to say yes, but she pauses a moment, listening. Then she whispers, "Not now. Maybe later."

Then he can hear, faintly, the level mumble of the television, and he knows it is the infernal son, still in the living room. It angers him, of course, but not so much that he can't hear the promise in what she has said.

Afterwards he considered whether she would go to a hotel with him, but it seemed a little too obvious, for the first time. So he planned to just invite her over to his house, which she had never seen. They would go out for a little candlelight supper, not too large, and then go over to his house for a nightcap.

And he did take her out for the little candlelight supper, but by the time he suggested the nightcap and tour of his house, she was tired and wanted to go home.

Though the Colonel was disappointed about the failure of this scheme, he was old enough to be very patient about sex. Another time, he thought.

But then, before long at all, Beatrice went back to the hospital. She lost her weight and became frail. Though she got out afterwhile and died, as she wished, at home, she wasn't able to go places much any more, and when she was, she wasn't in any condition.

The Colonel regretted this, of course, and not least because it meant the frustration of his particular hopes for her. The Colonel, being a sexual person, really values sex, insofar as he recognizes it. Still, he knew the decision had been up to her when she had had the chance; there was nothing more he could've done.

What bothered him most was what happened in the hospital. Beatrice was lying there, a skin-covered rack of bones but still with some strength in her. The Colonel went in to see her every day, and one day he bustles in wearing his red volunteer's jacket with the nametag that says Chief of Volunteers on it, and Beatrice is propped up on the raised head of the hospital bed: I see her in a pretty pink nightgown. Also, he had sent her an orchid—say, with pink fleshy lips like her own—which, confined in its water-filled green plastic tube, sat propped up on her bedside table in an empty drinking glass.

The Colonel says, "How are you today?" and she says she's all right.

"Well, tell me this," he growls. He is leaning over the bed, bracing a thick arm alongside her. "Is there anything you'd like that I can get or do for you?" This is the kind of thing the Colonel always says to Beatrice in the hospital, and sometimes she wants a magazine or for him to get the nurses to turn that other lady's TV down, or even for him to run out to the house and take care of something.

And this time, she has it all thought out. "I'd like," she says, "to do the silver waltz." She doesn't say "one more time," but that's what she means. The silver waltz is maybe a twelve- or twenty-four bar version of the regular waltz, with a lot of dips and turns, which the Colonel knows because the Colonel— whatever else he doesn't know about dancing—knows all the steps.

So the Colonel gets Beatrice up and into her new pink plush bathrobe and commandeers a wheelchair and gets her into that. At the last minute she has to wear the orchid, and there is a fuss involving nurses and safety pins, but in the end the Colonel just sticks the green plastic tube into the breast pocket of her bathrobe. Then he wheels her down the hall of the oncology floor to the elevator and out into the enclosed courtyard.

And there, in sight of ten floors of windows on all four sides, the Colonel takes Beatrice in his arms and they dance. Of course, they don't have any music, so the Colonel sings, and he can't think of any waltz except "The Merry Widow," which he doesn't remember the words to, but he hums the tune as well as he can, keeping the time as he guides Beatrice's big light frame through this complicated pattern of dips and turns that make up the silver waltz. Around and around they go, over the bright green indoor-outdoor carpet, among the potted Norfolk pines, to the Colonel's wordless approximation of the song. The orchid sticks out of Beatrice's pocket, the lacy neckline of the nightgown is a little like a ball dress, the long pink bathrobe flares like a train as they turn. On the final dip, the Colonel manages, without losing his balance, to bend over and kiss Beatrice lightly on the lips. He sees then how supremely fulfilled she is, as if she has completely forgotten there was ever anything else she wanted. And afterwards she was tired and went to sleep in the hospital bed, smiling.

This bothered the Colonel. Though he was glad to believe she was satisfied and later died content with her life, he couldn't understand what had happened to that other wish she'd expressed. He thought she must be kidding herself.

I told him my idea, but he couldn't buy it.

"Dancing!" he said. And when I hear him say this, I see him standing on the doorstep of the tan brick house, holding the bunch of flowers he knows is insignificant.

Around on the spiral of time, I boogie because Beatrice waltzed; I bounce straight up and down with my sweet man.

The Green Balcony

When she was little, Nina was like a cloud, here and there, which exasperated her mother. "Pay attention!" Nina's mother said. But where was this attention that had to be paid? In kindergarten the children cast their handprints, each in a white small pod of plaster of paris, and Nina stared at hers, for the exact connection it was supposed to have with her. She could not tell where she left off and the world took up.

She collected some as she got older, though not in any one place. Sometimes when she pumped her balloon-tired blue bicycle down the hot flat streets of their small town, she had a sensation of floating about eighteen inches out from her right shoulder. There seemed to be several of her: the one who saw or thought; the one who prayed; the one who wore red-and-white seersucker shorts and went into the bushes with Richard Possa and let him show her his thing. She was not any of them any more than any other. When at Vacation Bible School they cut out pictures of Martha and the three Marys and sheep and the Baby Jesus to paste up onto construction paper, she couldn't fit hers together into a picture of her own. She never thought about killing herself, but one time when she had climbed the rickety aluminum ladder of the municipal water tower all the way to the top to look out over the artificial branching of the irrigation ditches, the plowed red dirt sharply divided along section lines from the blond winter pasture, she thought how if the ladder were to pull away, as it seemed about to, and she fell and was smashed to bits, she would not be so different from the way she was then. In high school, she belonged simultaneously to the Future Teachers, the Future Nurses, and the Future Farmers.

Then she went away to college in the city, and all of this began to seem like an advantage. She could put on black stockings and go to bookstores and art galleries and cafes and have conversations. One time she was sitting at a wire-footed table on a wire-footed chair, and a man she knew, a young married man with a pale nose and a bitter compassion who had been her Freshman English instructor, insisted, "Catastrophe is the precondition of our lives."

And though she did not really know what he meant, she could reply in the language of the place, "Individually as well as collectively"—could go on and say, "My father used to lock me up in an abandoned chicken coop. My mother would come in to collect the eggs, though of course there weren't any eggs, and if I complained about what he had done, she would say, 'No, he didn't! No, he didn't!'" In fact, her family had never owned a chicken coop, but the story seemed as true as anything else.

The young man was bemused and looked at her with his head on one side. She wore silver earrings on which many little tips jiggled like the tips of crowbars.

And when she got tired of the simplicities of the intellectual life—it excluded a lot—she could run away from it. She could run to men with long thighs in Levis and get absorbed in what they were: Italian, Cajun, Mexican, Black; mathematician, politician, musician, plumber. Everybody but herself, it seemed, was something. The only trouble with this was that many would expect her to be, too, and not necessarily anything *she* had in mind.

Standing in the borrowed glare of a soundcheck, an elephantine man from Oklahoma with an earring in one ear stooped towards her in the posture of the very tall. "When I first met you," he said sadly, "I thought you were a Russian countess." The jukebox played, *She introduced herself as Sadie, but I think her name is really Eileen.*

Of course, when things got uncomfortable there, she could always slip away to the mission and hang around in a brown scapular-like garment with people who were absorbed in just being. Once she was sitting there on the scabrous yellow curb talking to a barefoot individual called the Dog Star Man. He was called that—she made up this explanation for herself, though she knew it wasn't the real one—because his toenails were long and curved downwards, like a dog's, and his eyes shone blankly, like the stars.

He had spoken of meditation, and she said to him, to see if she could believe it, "The diminution of the conscious faculties makes possible the expansion of the mental powers we call extraordinary."

He nodded vigorously, and his eyelashes beat like the wings of an insect. "Lives I've left," he said. "Apartments full of furniture I've walked away from."

And though this was not quite what she had meant, to be kind she let her own thought follow his, curving off after it like the track of a cosmic ray. Between them a pecan seedling grew straight up out of the storm sewer, already two or three feet visible.

"Only," she said, "I seem to live them all at once," and he laughed, but she was serious.

And there were other possibilities. One whole summer she rented a public garden plot carved out of a city park and cultivated tomatoes, which she canned. Wearing loose dresses suggestive of maternity she wiped the sweat off her face with a floursack cup towel and adjusted the jars in the water bath, feeling fertile and abundant. As the pantry shelves in the apartment filled up, however, this began to make her nervous. There seemed to be no future in it except to cook endless meals involving canned tomatoes.

Her professors, all men, gave them essays to write on the search for the self in the four novels we have read this semester, and Nina wrote obediently and got an A-minus, but this sort of question irritated her. Why would you, and how could you, search for something that was all over the place? In the end she graduated and fell into the most paralyzing depression.

She was waitressing in the humid city to feed herself and keep the shell of an apartment around her. Most of the time otherwise, she saw no reason to do anything any more than anything else. The place she rented was on the third floor of a gray concrete building half-covered by the vines that crawled dense and dark green on everything there. In these vines lived a kind of small greeny or browny lizard: she would see them on her way in as she paused with her hand on the rusted old front door knob; and at times the throats of the males would suddenly blow out into red-orange bulbs the color of pomegranate flowers. Something about this increased her despair.

When she got in from work she lay on the sofa with the stuffing coming out and stared at the ancient paper on the ceiling, which was water-ringed with multiple nonintersecting brown rings. It was August, and heavily, stilly, moistly hot, and she had shoved the sofa at an angle to catch the draft between the two doors. The apartment opened out onto a balcony, a splintery unpainted deck with an iron balustrade, itself cast in a pattern of vines. Over patches of rust coming loose, the balustrade had been painted a chalky green, and in a fit of desperate energy one day, Nina had gone out and bought a quart of paint in the dark green color of public restrooms and painted the deck of the balcony. A quart had not been nearly enough. The paint soaked right in, leaving the fibers of the wood exposed, though now green, to mock all the efforts she had ever made or would make. Sometimes, lying on the sofa, she picked up a book off the littered coffee table and paged through, though even a paperback pressed down on her chest so she could hardly breathe.

But one day when she did this—afterwards she couldn't remember which book it had been—she read how you could seek a vision for guidance in life. She wasn't sure exactly how it was supposed to provide that—she was just dipping in here and there. But why not, she thought, and in another of those desperate stabs at something that she could sometimes make, she decided to try to have a vision. She could not've said why she picked the green balcony to try on—only, perhaps, she needed to go someplace, and so she went there. She went into the kitchen and got two quart Mason jars, filled one with fresh water, and just as she was, in a pair of tattered shorts and sin-glet, went out onto the green balcony and sat down. First she folded her legs out, then in, and turned her pink soles up. Afterwhile, her feet went to sleep, and she stretched her legs out and leaned up against the concrete building.

Catty-cornered through the balustrade, she could see the back of another building, also with balconies. The people there seemed to use their balconies just like the people in Nina's building, as junk rooms or, with clotheslines running back and forth the length of them, to hang out wash. Nearer, she could see part of the trunk and the branches of a pecan tree that reached around the corner of the building, shading her some. Below, she knew but could not see, flowed the half-melted stream of an asphalt driveway from the parking lot out towards the street.

For three days and two nights she sat there, looking at what she could see, listening to the sounds of the neighborhood and the city. Every morning, cars left with the exact same se-quence of noises, beginning with the hard and prolonged gun-ning of an engine just before daylight. Much later, somebody directly below Nina came out and dropped what must've been the day's newspaper onto that balcony. Around noon, some-body in the building across the driveway began to practice the drums. At the end of the afternoon the cars came in, but rag-gedly, never in so regular an order as they left in, and every afternoon somebody slammed the door of a car or truck, shied what must've been a can at something, and missed: the can bounced off metal onto the pavement. First the twilight and then the darkness were illuminated by yellow parallelograms thrown out of people's windows, by the murmuring blue of television sets, finally only by the gray from streetlamps. Then you could hear the hum of the freeway and, way along in the night, a train that throbbed past, sounding closer than it was.

There she sat, eating nothing, drinking an occasional sip

of the water in the Mason jar; only at first had she peed into
the other Mason jar. She had not cared if people saw. She did
not care about anything except what she was doing. By the
third night, light-headed, she could see the bursts of radiation that rained down softly and continuously through the
atmosphere.

Glancing at the back of her hand where it rested on her
knee, she noticed a small scrape across one of the knuckles,
probably from the rough concrete of the building. When she
raised her hand to examine it more closely, she could see that
the top layer of skin had been torn away from a tiny triangular
patch. She stared at the torn edge of skin until it enlarged and
enlarged like a cartoon drawing in a textbook, and she could
see into it: a brickwork of little squarish cells with—buried
upside down in the top center—a sheathed spike. That was a
hair, she thought heavily. As she looked, she noticed that the
cells formed three indistinct layers. In the top layer, they were
flatter and clear and seemed to be coming unstuck from each
other, falling apart. In the middle layer, they were squarish and
gray and firmly mortared together. In the bottom layer, they
were tall and skinny, and the bottom surface was very uneven,
like a shoreline, with irregular inlets and peninsulas, and
while she watched, new cells were crowding up into exis-
tence from this wavy undersurface. She followed the barely
perceptible motion with which each layer was being pushed
up to become the one above it and the top layer flaked off
into dust.

Yes, Nina thought, she was that. And seeing, she knew that
she saw, and for a moment was both seer and seen.

Then she was sitting cross-legged on the green balcony
again in the gray light, staring at the back of her hand where
there was a little scrape. Her feet were asleep. There had been
a feeling she could not recapture. She knew she had had a
vision. Flesh, she thought, growth and dust; and though to've
had a vision at all was something, she felt vaguely disap-

pointed: what she recalled of it was just something everybody knew; it did not seem to be enough. She could go in now, she thought, but she didn't. Time passed. The bursts of radiation rained down through the atmosphere like heatless sparks.

The moon had sunk so it shone in among the leaves of the pecan tree, picking out surfaces here and there. Afterwhile she seemed to've felt before she noticed, among the umbrous shadows, a pair of reflecting eyes. Then she could see that they belonged to an owl-faced monkey, which lay in a crotch of the pecan tree where branches came together into a sort of platform nest. It lay head-down, like a baby on a crib mattress, and stared at her with steady bright eyes in the moonlight, and she stared back at it until she became it, looking over indifferently at her abandoned human body on the green balcony. She felt the hair growing in her hide, crooked her tail like a finger, smelled the pungent lacquer taste of beetles sizzling under nearby bark. Too, there bent over her, as in that moment it seemed always, another like herself, spreading the hairs in a polite ritual search for fleas, and then she was both of the monkeys as they chatted about conditions nearby in the words of their history, which was deep, if vague. And in all, she sang their song, with never a doubt about how it went.

We know, Nina thought, and about the past in us. Then she was herself again, sitting on the balcony in the late quiet night, trying to hold on to that confidence as it slid away. Her naked legs were stretched out in front of her in the moonlight, and she knew she'd had another vision, which in some way made one with the first, though she couldn't see how. She didn't think about going back inside then: she was onto something, she thought.

But even after it completed itself, she still didn't understand. The heavy night had cooled to lukewarm and stilled to a distant mechanical hum. The moon had set, and the dark flowed perceptibly towards morning. The interior of the tree, complicated by the ambient light, resembled a clearing in the woods, and Nina had just noticed this when into the clearing emerged the figure of a woman, as if on a walking trip; there was that purposefulness about her manner. She seemed middle-aged, neither young nor old, and she had on some pale drapery of visibly woven cloth—it might've been green, exposing a shoulder. Hovering there in the tree a little above the balcony, she looked like a woman in some painting Nina might've seen—the tranquil round face with its surface transparency of painterly flesh—only her features seemed to come from different paintings, so that she looked both familiar and not like anyone Nina had seen before. There was even a kind of family resemblance to Nina herself; the woman might have been some older relative—also in the concern she seemed to project for Nina.

And Nina knew that she was about to receive a message which would make sense of everything, but though she waited, breathing, there was no message. As she watched, the figure faded back through the branches the way it had come.

Then Nina was sitting on the green balcony in the ebbing dark, still with an odd feeling of reassurance. She was a little disappointed that she hadn't been able to sustain the vision long enough to receive its message, and she wondered what that would've been. But anyway, she had had her visions, and she was exhausted. The birds were twittering. Somebody in hard shoes walked around from in front and got into a car and raced the engine long and hard before pulling out. Nina got up and went in and went to bed and slept for nineteen hours.

Though she didn't understand about the woman, she continued to feel better. "Encouraged," she said lamely when she talked about this vision. She talked about it for some years and was surprised to find out how many people had had visions, apparitions, telepathies, and other unaccountable communications. She had conversations about these subjects until she was tired of them, but she never met anybody who could tell her who the woman in her vision was.

All the same, shortly after the vision she had managed to pull herself together, rather mechanically she thought at the time, had chosen a profession on the basis of her talents and interests (art history, she thought, putting her finger on it in the catalog), had gone to graduate school and gotten too busy to worry about a lot of things. She became. She became an iconographer, rediscovering her unfashionable reverence in religious artworks. She married, divorced, married again and had two children. She had more ordinary visions: the lost center panel of Gandolfo as it might have been, assembling itself against the blank wall over her desk, the man or child searching for her in his own dream.

And then it is one summer afternoon twenty years later. They are staying at a borrowed lakehouse that hangs high up off the old limestone riverbank like a balcony among the trees. She comes in from the hammering brightness outside to the dimness of the living room: at the doorway the two dogs jostle each other, stepping on her bare feet with their sharp toenails, then click on ahead over the linoleum as the screen door slams. Her arms are full of pale green scalloped squash from the garden. There is no one else in the house. The adolescent children have gone fishing; her husband will not be out from town until the evening.

Heading for the kitchen after the dogs, she catches sight of herself in the tarnish-spotted and dusty hall mirror, wearing an old threadbare one-shouldered sundress, once green, and the familiar image is suddenly strange with the memory: the woman from the green balcony. It was me, she thinks, the way I am today. Waves of locust rattle strike the house. She examines her face in the dim mirror. A middle-aged woman, like the woman in the vision, her tranquil round face sweaty from picking in the garden, which gives it that remembered look of surface transparence. With even the expression of kindly concern, as Nina has been thinking of squash and dinner. And it is a composed and variously achieved face.

Myself, Nina thinks, and what a way to find out, on a summer day so long later. In the kitchen the dogs drink water, dog tags jingling against the ceramic dishes, and she goes on in there through the dark pine-paneled hall, wondering about that time then and this time now and what happened in between. I became what I imagined? She supposes that's what most people would say. Or I somehow got a look at what I really always was?

Then there are images loose in time, a great flood of them in every odd conjunction. Down below the house the river is pulled slowly along the bottom by the current through the spillway. Green from reflections of trees, refractions of duck-weed, it spreads out there to make a section of lake.

Other Iowa Short Fiction Award and John Simmons Short Fiction Award Winners

1990
A Hole in the Language,
Marly Swick
Judge: Jayne Anne Phillips

1989
Lent: The Slow Fast,
Starkey Flythe, Jr.
Judge: Gail Godwin

1989
Line of Fall, Miles Wilson
Judge: Gail Godwin

1988
The Long White,
Sharon Dilworth
Judge: Robert Stone

1988
The Venus Tree,
Michael Pritchett
Judge: Robert Stone

1987
Fruit of the Month, Abby Frucht
Judge: Alison Lurie

1987
Star Game, Lucia Nevai
Judge: Alison Lurie

1986
Eminent Domain, Dan O'Brien
Judge: Iowa Writers' Workshop

1986
Resurrectionists, Russell Working
Judge: Tobias Wolff

1985
Dancing in the Movies,
Robert Boswell
Judge: Tim O'Brien

1984
Old Wives' Tales,
Susan M. Dodd
Judge: Frederick Busch

1983
Heart Failure, Ivy Goodman
Judge: Alice Adams

1982
Shiny Objects, Dianne Benedict
Judge: Raymond Carver

1981
The Phototropic Woman,
Annabel Thomas
Judge: Doris Grumbach

1980
Impossible Appetites,
James Fetler
Judge: Francine du Plessix Gray

1979
Fly Away Home, Mary Hedin
Judge: John Gardner

1978
A Nest of Hooks, Lon Otto
Judge: Stanley Elkin

1977
The Women in the Mirror,
Pat Carr
Judge: Leonard Michaels

1976
The Black Velvet Girl,
C. E. Poverman
Judge: Donald Barthelme

1975
Harry Belten and the
Mendelssohn Violin Concerto,
Barry Targan
Judge: George P. Garrett

1974
After the First Death There Is
No Other, Natalie L. M. Petesch
Judge: William H. Gass

1973
The Itinerary of Beggars,
H. E. Francis
Judge: John Hawkes

1972
The Burning and Other Stories,
Jack Cady
Judge: Joyce Carol Oates

1971
Old Morals, Small Continents,
Darker Times,
Philip F. O'Connor
Judge: George P. Elliott

1970
The Beach Umbrella,
Cyrus Colter
Judges: Vance Bourjaily
and Kurt Vonnegut, Jr.